PRAISE FOR

The Mannequin Murder

"This year's greatest literary surprise."

Dag og Tid

"The joy of storytelling practically cries out from the pages of this book."

Kulturkapellet.dk

"This is a prose cornucopia, a linguistic calorie bomb."

Klassekampen

"Ingvild Schade follows in the footsteps of Tarjei Vesaas and Ingvar Ambjørnsen, but with more extreme linguistic skill than them. . . . A daring and energetic storyteller."

Aftenposten

A delirious, darkly comic English-language debut from one of Norway's emerging literary talents

For your average fourteen-year-old, it would be a normal middle-class life: Father's a doctor, mother's an English teacher, a baby sister toddles aimlessly around the house in sagging diapers.

But Karsten is not like other fourteen-year-olds. Relentlessly curious and endearingly intense, he processes and narrates every element of the world around him in exhaustive, exhausting detail. Whether it's the intricacies of the optic nerve, how to gut a fish, or the queasy consistency of his mother's blackheads, nothing escapes his attention—and a grand story always waits just below the surface.

Not everyone finds his energy charming. Lately, a gang of neighbourhood boys have been sending him menacing letters, and even threatening to steal his metal detector. But Karsten has other things to worry about. When his father gives him a video camera to keep him busy, he immediately begins to spin a macabre mystery with himself as the hardboiled detective at its centre: the bloody corpse of a mannequin has been discovered in the compost and an investigation must commence, complete with filmed interrogations and a dramatic re-creation of the terrible crime itself—with his mother cast in the role of the murder victim.

Amid Karsten's rich and increasingly berserk fantasy, real life continues to intrude: a garden party at his family home draws near, his bullies demand satisfaction, and the eerie, lingering presence of his grandfather cannot be ignored.

Suddenly, one morning, Karsten's father asks him to say goodbye to his childhood home. An overnight bag is packed, and he is told they are leaving for a trip—and a new plan is set in motion.

Through gleefully ecstatic storytelling and a voice that recalls in equal measure the works of Kurt Vonnegut, Max Porter, and Anna Burns, Ingvild Schade has created an instantly unforgettable, one-of-a-kind character. You've never met a mind quite like Karsten's.

THE MANNEQUIN MURDER

THE MANNEQUIN MURDER

a novel

INGVILD SCHADE

TRANSLATED BY KARI DICKSON

STRANGE LIGHT

The Mannequin Murder was first published as
Bergverket by Cappelen Damm, 2019

First Strange Light edition published 2026

The authorized representative in the EU for product safety and
compliance is Penguin Random House Ireland, Morrison Chambers,
32 Nassau Street, Dublin D02 YH68, Ireland, https://eu-contact.penguin.ie

This translation has been published with the financial support of NORLA.

Library and Archives Canada Cataloguing in Publication

Title: The mannequin murder : a novel / Ingvild Schade ; translated by Kari Dickson.
Other titles: Bergverket. English
Names: Schade, Ingvild, 1987- author | Dickson, Kari, translator
Description: Translation of: Bergverket.
Identifiers: Canadiana (print) 20250325454 | Canadiana (ebook) 20250325462 |
ISBN 9780771018107 (softcover) | ISBN 9780771018114 (EPUB)
Subjects: LCGFT: Stream of consciousness fiction. |
LCGFT: Detective and mystery fiction. | LCGFT: Novels.
Classification: LCC PT8952.29.C53 B4713 2026 | DDC 839.823/8—dc23

Cover and interior design by Sid Watson
Cover art: Illustration by Sid Watson based on a reference image by yavyav; (grain) Uuganbayar, (grunge texture) inhabitant_b / all Adobe Stock
Typeset in Vendetta OT by Erin Cooper and Six Red Marbles
Printed in the United States of America

Published by Strange Light,
an imprint of McClelland & Stewart,
Penguin Random House Canada
320 Front Street West, Suite 1400
Toronto, Ontario, M5V 3B6, Canada
penguinrandomhouse.ca

1st Printing

Penguin Random House Canada

Afterthought for the reader

Thank you for joining Karsten for part of his journey toward uncertainty. Hope your respect for the lives of baby birds among the stones and thickets is further strengthened following this blowout.

Best wishes,
the author

I am Karsten. And that is the brick house behind the iron gates at the end of the road. And there we are, Father and I, on the muddy driveway. And this is the story that unfolds when Father opens the gate and we walk out between the leafy trees as the people we are: an older gentleman and his thunder-struck son. Say goodbye to the house, Father says. So we say goodbye to the house, with its grey facade and chalk-blue rooms. And goodbye to you, I say to the neighbourhood boys who stand lined up, sniggering, by the side of the road and ask where are you going, where are you going, as they punch the air with their small, freckled fists. I haven't the faintest idea, I reply. All I know is that Father has set me in motion, and I move one step further from all that I know every time I swing my back foot forward, then the other. Imagine, it's barely fifteen minutes since I woke up refreshed in my bed, stretched my arms to the ceiling and thought, now for a good breakfast before the school bell rings. Then, just as I part the curtains and open the bright day, my father pops his bearded chin around the door, says he's packed everything I need, that's to say toiletries, some underwear and an extra sweater for extra-cold days. Come on, Karsten, he says, time to hit the road, the world is waiting, so get your skates on, we need to get out of this house, away from this place, the dining room, the broom cupboard, the linen closet, the floorboards that creak as I hop around and pull on my denim trousers, in with the left foot, in with the right, just enough time to pop to the toilet in the corner where I quickly, quickly, quickly empty my bowels and bladder, and *swoosh*, run down the spiral staircase, slide on the soles of my socks, *thump thump thump*, Father grabs me by the arm, and with his knee pushes closed the door to his office, where he only yesterday barricaded himself behind a stack of patient records. Say goodbye to the house, he says. So we say goodbye to the house, the tables and chairs, lace tablecloths, crocheted bedspreads, the piano, the piano keys, a child's drawing of the sea and sky signed *Irene*, no unknown Irene, I'll have you know, my little sister Irene, my father's beloved chubby cherub, the one forever hanging and dangling around Mother, unless sitting in her Tripp Trapp chair throwing porridge at Father's beard, or at Mother who harrumphs, stands there shrivelled in the background, dust cloth in hand, hand on hip, because there are days when all she does is cry and gather up hair, because all that she touches turns to grey hair: the doorknobs, everything one touches, hasps and handles, lifts and holds, ladles, cutlery, cans, containers, carafes, the stool I was sitting on when I first saw the red threads in my eyes in a hand mirror. And there's more. There's the garden and corrugated iron shed. There's the climbing roses in front of said shed. There's the shaded pond behind the sprinkler where the statue of the Virgin stands. And the beech tree as well, with my name carved into the bark in a heart. Not to forget the pots of pansies on the flagstones by the front door. Things that can really only be called decorative nonsense, I say to the neighbourhood boys, who've clearly chosen to follow us part of the way. Just some silly nonsense in your peripheral vision, really, I say, and they grin greedily, feasting on the uncertainty that Father has now fostered in me. Well, it's possible that I look a little lost as I walk, but actually I enjoy whetting my wit on guessing games, puzzles, labyrinths, finding my way to whatever is missing, via peepholes, hidden doors, underpasses, causal links. And for want of any better alternatives, I choose the retrospective approach—I beg your pardon? That's to say, I get my bearings by studying in detail what we're leaving behind before eliminating irrelevances one by one, saying thanks for now, dear expedient means, and the better my grasp on where this is going, the more the underlying chaos subsides. Though I should perhaps not be too detailed here, as pedantic precision and elaboration tend to complicate rather than clarify. I've tripped up on that before, investigated and assessed all possible angles, twists and turns and shadows, only to stagnate in a soup of hitherto truths that have been boiled to death by reason, which, I'm afraid to say, ultimately only highlights the limits of reason. And this limitation of reason is the very reason I never dare make brash statements about anything—yes, even if it's a matter of simple facts, simple sums, the four elements, the three primary colours, for example, why red feels intrusive, why blue is so absorbing, why the golden concept *before* always ends up in the background veiled by, oh, poor Mother there in the window, waving, holding Irene's hand, forcing Irene's hand to wave like her own, Mother's waving hand, they blow kisses from their fingers, doodles, hearts and rubber stamps that will follow me into eternity—sheesh, I say, but really, I mean yes, Father smiles without shame, unlike me, I pull my jacket collar up to hide two burning ears. Ah, I yawn, opening my mouth wider, as though unperturbed by the neighbourhood boys who comment on how fast my blush is spreading. Talk about being a caricature of yourself. But let me tell you, anything else would be utterly impossible as long as I'm being followed by such practical, rational types whose only goal is to stop me in my endeavours with scornful definitions and concepts. They call me the shrimp, among other things, I who am the best all-rounder in sports; they also call me the shit specialist, based on a single incident, not something I generally do, but a single episode, and it certainly doesn't help to answer back, as it only results in futile discussions, misunderstandings, schisms. There was, for example, the time I caught them peeing in the raspberry canes, tinkling amber-yellow pee that echoed in my ears and formed arcs between the berries, that shone like tiny rainbows when sunbeams broke out at an angle from a crack in the clouds. Have you been saved? they asked. Eh, I think so, I said, and then they shot me with finger guns. I said that's enough now! That you can't just say or do something then distance yourself from it in the same breath! They ran off, knees high across the lawn, jumped over the fence and hid under the neighbour's terrace, where they crouched with their hands over their mouths, holding their breath, until I eventually found them with the help of my metal detector, which beeped ever louder as I got closer to their shiny belt buckles. Found you, I said sternly, and asked them politely to scram. Or rather, when I think about it, I simply pointed out that the detector had worked as it should, and that I'd just got it for my birthday, as ordered. How much did it cost? Well, let's just say that we didn't celebrate a child's birthday that summer, I had in fact turned fourteen, and I'd made sure to inform Mother in good time before the big day that toys are something you give to children, whereas teenagers prefer proper presents, not pretend-things, but functional tools that actually work. We're talking, of course, about the cutting-edge-technology type of metal detector, the price of which promises that it will not only differentiate between different kinds of metal, but will also indicate the distance to any metal objects in and out of the sensor's sensitivity field. Yes, I generally get what I want, what I point to, no matter how much it costs. You spoil me, I often say to Mother. But you deserve all that you get, Mother replies. Imagine. Irene does too. Even a Mercedes when you can drive, says Father. That's a promise. I'm also fortunate enough to have a spry grandfather who, every second Sunday, contributes to my treasure trove of coins, glass, precious stones, most recently an amethyst and before that a piece of calcite with small cubes of pyrite which, if I'm not remembering wrongly, I held out in front of me when the boys finally crawled out sniggering from their cowardly hideaway. I said okay, okay, but before you take another step closer, I want to remind you that it's seven against one. Then I asked if they thought it was fair to sabotage other people's berry bushes—do you really think that's okay? I was about to say hallelujah for feelings of responsibility, because they make us all look good, as do feelings of humility, but my father interrupted with a shout from the window—remember that wisdom doesn't argue, Karsten, it reveals. And well might he say that. But Mother says it better. Mother has said that I should stand in front of people like a silent mirror until everything just pours out of them. Never say more than is necessary, is what she actually said. It piques their curiosity, Karsten. Piques their curiosity. Be a perfect example of inquisitive openness. An energy field of the unspoken, Karsten. And thus, on Mother's advice, I intend to follow Father in silence beneath the leafy trees, stare in awe at the road, a road with a roof of leaves, a road between houses that turns into a bumpy gravel track when the houses disappear around the next corner and all that can be seen is fields, hillsides, a kennel, the odd remote bible school where students sit on wooden chairs and study opaque texts. So it's simply a question of when the neighbourhood boys will lose interest. I reckon they'll get as far as the doghouse—hehe. Or wait, I take that back, because dogs are happiest when they're free, Mother says, and releases them whenever she hears me think. Well, excuse me and my tendency to view others as morally responsible beings, but then, as mentioned, I think the boys should not go unpunished for certain things. For example, the way in which they carry on, in the scree behind the house. I mean, goodness, they use crowbars to loosen big boulders which then crush poor weasels and small birds. I've also seen them use a jack, a big old jack that can lift up to twenty tons with the help of a pump. They even boast about it, want me to marvel at its collapsibility, scissor arms made with vises, crank handles, spare parts and so on. But, good heavens, all those spare parts are no guarantee that the technology is cutting-edge or, gracious,

requires much expertise to use. Really there isn't much more to understand than that the bottom needs to stand on something flat. The boys usually solve this by levelling a slab stolen from our driveway, with gravel and sand. And, well, the contraption is then positioned on the slab, before they start the pump. And I don't know how often I've been lying on the grass reading, and maybe dozed off, when *bang*! Yet another of these explosions! The smell of gunpowder! I feel the dust in my eyes!
I sometimes even catch myself longing for bad weather. Oh, how I long to see rain being chased across the windowpanes. Let it drip, I say, let it fall, trickle from the gutters, spill over, octagonal umbrellas, give me thunder, lightning, a cloudburst that sounds like chronic bronchitis, yes, thank you, it's called yearning. Yearning for rain. Oh, to see them slip on the stones. I'm so glad that I drink the rain. I walk with my mouth open like a cup—*gulp!* Because that's how I cool myself down, practise forgiveness as any thoughts of revenge are washed away, leaving light and peace—or what do you think, Father? Do you know of a better way? Should I rather just shrug and

walk on? Say thanks for now and goodbye? Right, I'll do just that, Father. I'll say farewell to the neighbourhood boys. Farewell to those mouth-breathers who never fail to choose the easiest way out. Goodbye to you. May some generous person have mercy on you, or pray that by the grace of God you end up on the right side and not inside the criminal system, behind walls, in cells, where stepmotherly police officers apparently give out candy when they want you to talk during questioning, and spout clichés about vicious circles. That the shameful seek out the shameless, for example. Female cunning, they call it. Chewing a wine gum with you. Icky, says Mother. Tent-breath, says Father. No, stay well away. Get some education. Yes, let's hope that education will knock some manners into a couple of you yet. Only the best end up in health care, says Father, who's a doctor, of course. Anything is better than prison, says Mother, who's an English teacher. Well, most people end up in warehouses, I reckon, thinking of the silent, unsentimental types who do work that anyone can do, only faster, without eating, they don't need to, only drink water on their break, apparently it's called a trance in English, Mother says, and they're actually worthy of respect, because they're real men, and real men never make a fuss, never victimize others, Father says. So, let's hope that these boys, given time and maturity, will prioritize a decent life over messing about in the dirt all day. Manual work might be the thing? Sorting trash? Would have to be heavy tasks in that case, lifting, lugging. But! Heavy work is not to be scorned. It's a tough environment, according to insiders. Do they know what discipline is, in practice? Seriously. As soon as they walk into that warehouse, they'll have to lose all their bad habits—throw them down like a sour, brown cloth, preferably strip back to basics, the pure noiseless essence, the fundamental formula and original contents, where their souls no doubt will prove to be a silly by-product of some chemical brain activity, psychological slime, suited to what they do, taunting God and confusing science and materialism, method and ideology, the microscope and the cross, there's a fundamental difference, remember, the microscope enlarges the smallest detail, whereas the cross symbolizes the eternal picture and, thus, is on such a high level of abstraction that it can never be understood by these heirs of the Enlightenment's so-called rationalism, no, don't ask me why anyone would want to restrict themselves to the sterile reality of arithmetic, geometry, and quadratic equations that, haha, certainly won't enrich them as they trudge over the gravel like impoverished slobs with no will, none at all, no, they have no aim in life other than to consume energy drinks, and perhaps get themselves a switchblade, an amusing toy to play with, though not necessarily to attack people, because there's a limit, and that's crossing the line beyond the limit, and by the way I'm not allowed to be sloppy with idioms at home, because that's what it's like at home. To be fair, though, Father now says that rule no longer applies, in fact, there are no rules, because rules restrict one's capacity for adventure, and from now on almost everything will be constructive regurgitations anyway, of what we call memory, then he turns to the right, past Grandpa's house, and soon we're walking by the glass veranda where the old man sits confused in his wing chair, waiting for Mother to invite him for coffee, he coughs, thumps his chest, and I wave to him but he doesn't see us, we disappear too quickly, full speed up the hill behind the churchyard, Father times us, wants me to walk faster—why? Well, I may well wonder. As though I don't already have enough to wonder about. For example, right now I'm wondering who it was who said that memory has more to offer than ingenuity. Yes, that's the truth, and finally we're onto the subject (after the chemical elements) that interests me the most, which is memorization, and I can get very heated about it, I can say b-b-because the fact is that our autobiographic and episodic memories are continually being changed and re-created and adapted to what seems to be reasonable in the moment we bring them up. Scary stuff. Especially the fact that we stumble through loads of strange events that bleed into each other to create what are called hybrid memories—shhh! I say, and decide that forthwith the neighbourhood boys will be remembered as seven faded background figures, the kind that always appear in old-fashioned group photos, eyes bulging with malnutrition, anemia, goitre, crowbars pointing to the ceiling, that's how they will stand and stare blankly, far back in my silent soul, because now I just want to run without baggage, with the wind in my curls in my mouth my eyes my nose, sprint after my father—Father, I'm coming! Because, the fact is, I have nothing against being one of two carefree lads drifting along country roads, side by side, sleeping in hostels and inns, chatting with fellow travellers while we eat in taverns, square meals, we lean across the table toward a good story, tall tales, witty, rude and, goodness, sensitive to colours, feelings, thoughts about why colours describe feelings like feelings describe colours—imagine, someone might say, that the emerald is green, not with envy, but with trace elements of chromium or vanadium, exactly, this is, in short, poetry, we all agree to that, couldn't have said it better ourselves, we say, and so it continues with clapping and shouts and turns of phrase so that no one can stick to their favourite subjects, there's barely a chance to say more than whatever it might be before it's twisted into something unfamiliar in someone else's mouth, because that's how meals should be, we should not want to leave the table, we should want to stay there all night and get so close to these strangers that they feel like family, yes, haha, we may even invite them home, we can't wait, we invite them home immediately so we can h-h-have a good time all over again, repeat the whole meal, be it meat, potatoes, and thick, dark gravy made with devotion and emotion by Mother, who knows how to flavour it with brown cheese, beef stock, mustard, malt, chopped herbs, blackcurrant, and a bit of colouring if necessary, so that it's so tasty that the guests will suck it like sweets, purring with pleasure, rolling the gravy around their tongue, while Father praises Mother to high heaven, what a goddess she is, that he met her at a spa hotel, of all places, and oh-ho-ho he has to laugh, he just knew that he had to have her when she (the young teacher) slipped out from under the waterfall, slowly, first a hand, then a foot, then her slim, pale body, because that is how, in that given order, she came toward him (the older GP), he who quickly dried his beard with a terry-cloth towel and, goodness, had to lean against the wall, because good lord, seeing her with her loose wet hair—fair, shiny, long-long hair—made his head spin, so blond that it was white, pitch-black when it was wet, when the water ran in trickling stripes down her breasts, thighs, she shook her hair in slow motion, then swung it forward and back, flicked it against her back hard as a whip! And he could barely answer when she said hello, that she recognized him, even remembered his name, because they were not completely new to each other, no, they'd been introduced at a party a couple of weeks ago, by mutual friends, but it was really here at the spa hotel that they discovered that the chemistry between them worked, and they left the place hand in hand, like two united halves of one Karsten. A good boy, they say. A good boy. And yes, it's true that I'm considerate, that I want to contribute to the happiness of this world. But I can also be a pest at times, just so that's said. I have, for example, a habit of throwing my duvet and pillow on the floor, which means that my mother has to pick up my mess, to make my bed with strictly aesthetically considered symmetry. And she is so tired during the day, and has to carry Irene around, too. Great piles of English tests have recently grown on the living room table. There was porridge on the Sunday tablecloth the last time I looked. In the hall, unopened letters lay strewn across the tiles. And the other evening, when I was taking my metal detector out from behind the coats, I knocked over a plastic bag full of soiled diapers. MUUUM! I shouted, because all the jackets stank of hydrogen sulphide, they needed to be washed and aired—where was she? Mother? Having looked in all the rooms on the ground floor, the living rooms, kitchen, I tiptoed upstairs and peeped in the first open door. There she was, oh dear, sitting on the edge of the bed again, bent forward in her bobbly nightdress—what was she doing? Pulling the ugly grey hairs from her fringe? Oh, Mother dear, I said—what do a few grey hairs matter in your thick mane of golden curls?

That's alright for you to say, she said with a sigh to the full-length mirror, an old grey English teacher, is there anything worse? I suggested it might be healthier for her to direct her anger outward—to link her own problems to systemic failures, a society that places too great an emphasis, and contradictory demands, on beauty and what to do when it fades and becomes brassy. Remember that you're keeping pretty well, I said, and hurried to compare her with Grandpa, who has a hearing aid and a stick. And speaking of Grandpa, he's more than forty years older than her, but no less lively for that, he walks past our house every day, for God knows what reason. Do you want some coffee, I ask, and he'll say he doesn't want to intrude, no, he's happy as long as he can stand on the road and watch his daughter from a safe distance, when she's having fun in the garden, cutting the hedge, she snips off the branches that stick out and Irene gets the twigs in her face, pollen on her eyelashes, and Mother laughs, no, no, no, you're not allowed to pick the buds, poppet. On a good day, Mother is the first thing I see from my bedroom window, her smile among the branches, she's comfortably crouched in the undergrowth, talking to the plants, chit-chatting about this and that and anything that comes to mind. Because Mother isn't always tired and sad, generally she's glowing, full of enthusiasm, whether she's weeding, watering or just warbling around like a happy bird with green stains on her blouse, roses in her cheeks, her hair in a bun, loose in the shower, flat on the pillow, in braids in the morning, running in her gammon-pink clack-clack-clack shoes across the flagstones. They say that Mother is so easily excited, so easily distracted, imagine, I could be sitting on her hip only to *whoosh* be thrown up in the air to the neighbourhood boys, then she splashed a splash of water on her face, dabbed some lipstick on her lips, and threw her arms around Father, threw herself at him, she wanted children, more children, rolling her Rs, morrre childrrrren, lots of childrrrren, a boy with bounce, and a demanding bundle with splash-blue eyes, let's call her Irrrene, or Svanhild, initially they preferred the name Svanhild, but couldn't risk their daughter being taken for a fool, no, let's make love, darling, she said, and they made love high and low, as loudly as they could, used the word love, to love, to be two lovers who loved each other loudly between the sheets so that one caress became another became the next and the next until they were entwined in each other, or more spun into their own little web in the all-encompassing spin of the universe. Oh, my love, he said. My saviour, she said, and curled her many thin legs around him. But that is according to Father, to be fair—that's to say, I'm copying his style, Father with his dizzying descriptions. I've heard it said before: I have Father's voice and Mother's hair. It's the language of longing, Father says. And it's the listener's job to fill the blind spots with their own assumptions. A declaration of trust. There's a dangerous number of places for impatient boys to play, he chuckles in front of me. And all of a sudden, he's chatty, let me tell you, and I who thought we'd each walk in our own world, but now he keeps looking over his shoulder to make sure I'm keeping up, wants me to respond, says he wants to engage me in proper conversation, as an equal sparring partner, because, indeed, I am qualified, he says, and praises my eloquence, that I can argue, discuss and reason, and not least, that I'm completely honest, though I mustn't let it go to my head, he says, having long since warned me against becoming big-headed, in the worst case contacting the National Registry and asking to change my name to something strange, to call myself something abstract, like a weather phenomenon or a species. No, better to look around, Karsten, he says, a reminder not just to stare down at the toes of one's shoes all the time, but to look up at the hillsides on the horizon, to take in the landscape, its deep clefts and scrubby ridges. Look at the forest in front of us, Karsten. Look at the sky. See the light on the fields. See the people in the bus shelter, see them smiling, wishing us a good trip, Karsten. Just look at it all, Karsten, he says cheerfully, and I have to say his beard is looking unusually bouncy, a red bushy beard that curls in on itself in damp weather. Just look, he says, and shakes a branch so the rowanberries rain down on his boots. That's where I walk to work, he says, and points over the field to some stone steps with a handrail for support when it's icy, as it was this winter, he says, and brrrr was it cold, he remembers, snow on the trees, and knowing him, he counted his steps as he walked, down the ice-caked steps, followed his feet, to and from work, a warm, clean medical centre where he shook the snow from his coat over the shoe rack and gave his patients in the waiting room a quick wave before he acknowledged with a nod the shadows dancing over the walls and ceilings, the floor that creaked. Because Father is a man of detail, the sort who has enough energy to search amongst the fragments, splinters, in the pores, in fact he can smell what is wrong with his patients, if it's streptococcus, a urinary infection, hernia, hiccups, or any other common condition or symptom it might be. It's forbidden to call people cripples, he really cares about them, takes his time, examines every little surface, reminds them to change their toothbrush between antibiotic treatments, or to boil their toothbrush if they can't afford to buy another, and to remember to eat every three hours, to walk to work, to walk to somewhere, to get some daylight in their eyes, to bite a pencil hard between their teeth if they are unable to smile, to try at least to look forward, to celebrations, holidays, birthdays, a glimpse of continuity or identity or something. He always asks about the quality of their sleep, often quotes a verse or two about mist, embroidery, whatever the case, you still have to do what's most important, he says firmly, making demands of them out of respect, they must surely be able to do that, he says, remember that you've been made to master frustration, people, that we all should be able to delay satisfaction, plan, stick to agreements, preferably see pain as an opportunity, not just a mental short circuit, but an intricate passage out of the complication, the only way out in fact, he says, and, shuffling forward in his chair, asks them to open wide, one by one, stick out their tongue, hold it against the roof of their mouth and then release it quickly with a *click.* And that makes them laugh, it's important to laugh, he says, he knows how to release pressure, take a slow approach, and then, Bob's your uncle, burst the balloon with a gentle *click*, well, easy enough for him, because we're talking about a man whose social skills are quite simply exemplary, wild at parties, generous and direct in his dealings with anyone, serves gin and tonic in vases, even though he doesn't drink himself, might occasionally have a glass of wine with Mother when they're alone and being romantic, but never with anyone else, doesn't need a lubricant to cheer and dance, but keeps an eye on everyone, that everyone has something in their glass, quite impossible to dislike, say his friends, a legion of friends who clap in unison when he shows slides in the basement, beautiful pictures, truly beautiful slides, because Father is a professional, in everything, interested in all kinds of things, doesn't hesitate to get involved in new public debates where he sparkles with incisive arguments, solid sources and wit, and wins every time, of course, no matter what it's about, because he touches something fundamental, topples opponents by talking from the distance of hindsight, a perhaps condescending but charismatic distance, in the way that only a worldly man can, a man with a happy home life, with no other problems in fact, who never has to put in too much effort, but loves his wife, is loved by his wife, uses the word love, to love, to make love so much that one falls through the bed and down into the water in the pond under the tree, to swim under the tree, to be requited, united in most things, that marriage is organized around coitus, in fact a lot can be resolved if one gets the hang of conflict management in the home, and we all have a lot to learn here, because Father and Mother have made reconciling conflicting interests in a peaceful, magnanimous manner into a sport, we're talking no shouting, no fitful scuffles, nothing, they respond to heckling with politeness, and in challenging periods they look through the photo album, laugh at the bridal veil, Father in a top hat, the two long-necked witnesses, very serious, Grandpa's speech that lasted thirty-four minutes without pause, the kissing bride and groom, her feeding him cake, licking the cream from her fingers, they kissed with tongues, kissed as if there were no one else in the room, like living in a love letter, they smelled of lavender, a breeze in the curtains, Father had butterflies in his beard, found Mother in the wardrobe hanging on a clothes hanger like a dress, her feet dangling, he said being with you is fun and games all the way, and they laughed together, had so much fun together, especially when they showered, gurgled water, pressed their bodies against each other, their buttocks squashed flat against the shower door, flat and white, skin slapped against the tiles, soap foam in their ears, a shower of white lace down over their shoulders, their backs, he swung her around, called her a minx when she suggested champagne, oh go on, she said, because they had even more to celebrate, she had just completed her master's in English, he had a five-page spread in a medical journal, an article on comfort, how to comfort a wilful scamp, their faces were luminous, shining, as though the windows moved around with the sun, rotated the house to face the sun, it's all about commitment, the fair division of responsibility, they held hands in the washing-up bowl, they shook out rugs together, Father stood ready with the towel on the outside step while Mother washed me in the sink, he put on the duvet cover while she plumped the pillows, he made the food, she took out the trash, and he was happy to look after the laundry while she fed me with a spoon, her hand shook a little, spilled soup on my pyjamas, but you couldn't call it neglect, it was only a lukewarm splash, a mere slip of the hand, one has to forgive her, we all make mistakes, and remember that he who makes no mistakes does little else either, a good maxim for life, might be worth collecting some, or lots of isolated quotes by the great freethinkers, and well said too, yes, good good good, yes on what is wise and what is the total opposite, in other words, stupid, says Father. So yes, like my father, I say that a pithy quote can take you a long way, that there's plenty of opportunity in all the chatter, but be warned that people are always ready to attack whoever says it, because they want you to fall flat on your face, because if you don't fall flat on your face they'll have to reassess their own choices! he shouts from way up ahead. Remember, no one enjoys doubting their own judgment, Karsten. He slows down, apparently out of breath, says that it looks like I'm limping a little, dragging my back foot. And who are they? I ask. The ones who want me to fall flat on my face? Surely they can't be very happy, Father? The ones who want me to fall flat on my face? In fact, I can't think of anyone other than the boys back there, that band of rascals from the neighbourhood who sent me written threats because they can barely speak. And by the way, I paid most attention to the one that came sailing over the hedge recently during the holidays:

TO KASTEN. WE DONT LIKE YU. WE THINK YUR STUPID. FROM THE ENMY

This was sent as a paper plane over the hedge on a very ordinary, partially clouded summer's day. Mother was taking off her gardening gloves when the letter came flying on the wind in a trajectory that Irene followed wide-eyed, up and down, until it landed at my feet. I was possibly overly suspicious of others' motives and intentions at the time, but between the lines of what the enemy had quite literally communicated, I read an unpleasant hidden warning to be extra careful from now on, that I should not feel safe in my own garden anymore. And so I stayed indoors as much as I could. In fact, I was at the point where I wanted to barricade myself in my room with the double-barrelled shotgun from the shed. And now the small sink behind the wardrobe certainly came into its own right, as I'd have to have drinking water, as well as snacks, candles, lots of snacks. But a shotgun was out of the question, Father said, even if it was empty of cartridges. No, absolutely not. Please, I begged. No way, said Father. But I could borrow his video camera, just for something to do, as he put it. Well, if you insist, I said, as though I hadn't nagged him to borrow it every day since he'd got it as a gift from his patients on his fiftieth birthday. And it was a good camera, expensive, waterproof, the kind with countless settings and a gold knob you could twiddle to zoom the picture in and out. Well, I made myself comfortable on the windowsill so that I could try all the different effects. I zoomed in on a bird on the washing line. I zoomed in on the orange sunlight shining through the leaves of the beech tree. With a click, I changed the filter and the light became ultraviolet. The natural light was better, I quickly realized, because the eerie atmosphere couldn't really be filtered by such technical wizardry from one side or the other. I shook the camera to make the Virgin statue tremble. Then I tried to film Irene in such a way that Mother's grey braid did not appear in the picture, and for a moment it almost looked as if the wee darling were toddling about on her own in the wind and pollen and—what? No, don't ask me how, but in a surprising leap of association, this little scene inspired the idea that I could make an intricate murder mystery, something to keep me busy and make the summer pass. I imagined a young, virile, yet experienced detective going through the garden with a fine-tooth comb in search of a body. He's just about to stop for the day, pack up his things, put his metal detector back in its case, when goodness, he sees something disturbing on the compost heap—and what is it? A hand holding an apple? He digs down in the compost, he throws rotten vegetable peelings and grass to the side in desperation, and gradually she, the victim, appears. She has the same face as the Virgin, the same ancient smile. And from her hand falls a worm-ridden Gravenstein apple.

Exactly.

Gravenstein, Gravenstein, I mumbled, only to discover that the word stimulated my salivary glands, in the same way as stainless steel, Peter Piper, intestinal tubes, washbowls and triangular particles. Exactly. I had found my calling in life,

I would certainly say that. And the neighbourhood boys could laugh at me as much as they liked, I said out loud out the window—they're welcome! Then I closed the curtains, turned on the desk light and put the camera to my eye, zoomed in on a passport photograph of my mother as a girl, beyond unrecognizable. I studied the face in detail, the tiny squares in her skin. Suspicious, I thought, and sighed, as though exasperated, as I, knowing myself, used my free hand to coax the edge of my underwear out from between my buttocks. It's a bit stuffy in here, Father said from the door. Get out, I said curtly, and immediately regretted it, because now I couldn't ask him if I could throw beetroot juice all over the gravel, so I had some blood to examine. Damn. I got a notebook out from the desk drawer, scribbled down lots of words that Mother forbids me to use. Whore, for example. W-H-O-R-E. Whoremonger, as well. Tralala, The Forbidden Eraser song. *Want a you-know-what that quietly erases all I've said and meant and thought and considered and done.* The evidence was scant. Thus far I had little more than my mother's passport photo, and a hair that must have left a black hole in the victim's scalp, judging by the drop-shaped root. Possibly. No matter, I thought—from what little I have, I can spin a whole web of scenarios, contradictions, hmm, by investigating anyone who is potentially involved, even, for example, the victim's peripheral friends, with their somewhat vague inside perspective. Mannequins, the whole lot of them, by the way. Drama queens. Contraceptive pills. The kind who chew chewing gum when they speak, wear ridiculously large capes and hats. I put the passport photo in a plastic folder. With sticky tape, I attached the hair carefully to the margin of the page where I would later transcribe my interviews with the victim's shocked friends who, gracious, couldn't speak because they were crying so much. I noted that their tears flowed in grey arcs from their eyes, that the detective, with some reluctance, handed them tissues, three glasses of water. Everything had to be recorded, everything everything everything that these liars might think of to deceive me. No, I felt no sympathy. And it certainly wasn't for want of trying, as I would spend hours trying to break through their protective armour that seemed to make them immune to any unpleasantness, but which in reality stood in the way of a healthy path in life, good relations, I said, which made them break down again, one fell to the floor, racked with sobs, clinging to the root of her nose. Where were you that evening? I asked. And your friendship, is it some kind of sect-like sisterhood with secret initiation rites? No, nothing shocks me, I made sure to say. I've seen it all, I said, heard it all, my last case was a sad case where an innocent man had been imprisoned with nothing more than a bag of flour, some turnips and half a cabbage. But these were intelligent girls, bright intelligent girls, I realized, so I had to tread carefully here, not dig, but rather coax and manipulate with digressions, captivating anecdotes, such as the edifying tale about the blind, deaf fool who, after a successful operation, went to a strip club to fully appreciate his regained sight. But what he should have done, I said, was to look into the eyes of his ever-faithful guide dog. A Dalmatian. Yes, you could say it was beating around the bush, a burning bush, even, that emits ominous sparks and smells. Boo! I said, having told them about a couple of everyday outdoor experiences, hit the table with my fist, the mannequins jumped and I asked them straight why they were lying, what they were hiding, I wanted to know what they were keeping inside, what difficult thoughts they tussled with in the dark of their bedrooms, when they all lay apart in their separate beds and wondered if it was only the self and its conscience that is alone, so utterly alone. Come on, girls, what happened that evening? There was a damp chill in the air, they sniffed. Were they at a club? At a club? Yes, a club. They were on the dance floor having fun, keeping their eyes on the patent leather shoes that walked to and fro as they counted the beats together, when suddenly the fourth friend, the victim that is, unexpectedly said goodbye to the others. Without saying why. No one asked. And after that, the victim disappears without a trace, nothing is seen of her for months, until the detective finally, having searched every nook and cranny in the neighbourhood with his detector, finds her mutilated body in the compost heap, holding a Gravenstein apple.

Gravenstein, Gravenstein, what more do we know?

Well—we know that the victim lived in the city, or to be more precise, in a young woman's bedsit with shrieks and squeals, hair-removal cream, sanitary towels, lacy underwear, bottles that broke behind the creaking radiator that was irresponsibly close to laundry baskets full of flammable nylon stockings. There were buzzing flies in the room, on the walls, inside the fridge where various sauces were growing mould on the shelves. On a corkboard above the metal-frame bed, she had, in an attempt to bring order to her erratic life, lots of Post-it notes, a reminder to collect a dress from the dry cleaner, a telephone number, a job advert from the newspaper. Secretary for a property development company, something like that. She had celebrated prematurely, bought herself a pencil skirt and laid it out nicely on the duvet at the end of the bed. Makeup smears on the sheet suggested bulimic tears, remains of bulimic vomit, that she spent too much time in bed, often bent double with stomach pains, indeed, having force-fed herself like a goose. And this, this on luxury foods stolen from the grocery store by the station where, according to the owner, she was wont to pour warm sherry conserve into her coat pockets, ice cream, pâtés, veal medallions, cod, which she rinsed down with Riesling, only to throw it all up in the toilet without flushing. If one is to believe the psychiatrist, this was a way to centre herself, feel her connection to the earth, because when she wasn't stuffed, she flew out of her body up to some pastel-coloured astral cloud, which was not of this world. Don't leave me! she cried to the psychiatrist, whimpered through her worn teeth, an incoherent, dark noise. She wasn't grounded. She was in a transition period, the psychiatrist believed. At the point of realizing that to feel special is just a normal way to deny death, he said. She had even admitted to him that she confused beauty and competition, that her competitive streak was like a blindfold. A kind of tangled web of glitter and slag, she said. The mornings were worst, when the alarm clock filled her with fear, the thought of solipsism, a buzzing pressure from the inside that produced the outside, misty childhood memories, stepfathers with handlebar moustaches, rental cars. Oh. She flung on a knee-length dressing gown, soft, fluffy fabric, shivering, she made a syrupy black drink of water, sugar and instant coffee. It was snowing outside. She pulled a couple of ready-rolled cigarettes from a mouldy tobacco pouch on the counter, put one in her mouth and the other under the strap of her bra. Took the coffee with her over to the window where she peered out, like someone short-sighted, at the falling snow and the empty street that narrowed to a point at the end. Here the buildings grew together in a haphazard manner via tiny gutters, fire escapes and high-voltage power lines. Like a reflection of her twilight mood, I noted. A perfect mould of the inner life inside her bony girl's body. A happier soul with an optimistic outlook might have seen the flowering pot plants that sparkled so magically on the snow-clad balconies. Thoughts can be like a herding call. Her constant negative thoughts attracted trouble from the lower realms, rats, rotten men whose bodily fluids ran in her veins, saliva, DNA, pigeon shit, sperm cells, she recognized the symptoms, slight nausea, sore nipples, the characteristic pressure in her pelvis, a hankering for liquorice, intense, titillating, the smell of gasoline, she was pregnant. Yes. Pregnant. I wrote PREGNANT in double felt-tip letters, filmed the letters from left to right until the whole word was in the frame. Perhaps she wanted to keep the child against the father's will? He was probably unemployed, couldn't afford the child maintenance payments and felt that he wasn't being heard, that he was talking to a wall, because she, she, she was going to have the child no matter what, he could say what he liked, she stood firm, had decided to have the child, with or without his support, even if all she had to offer was poverty in a bedsit, the laundry basket as a cradle, foundation instead of diaper rash cream, if she had to patch together nylon stockings to make onesies, use the ashtray as a porridge bowl, or thicken the porridge with blush—would he allow his child to grow up in such conditions? No, of course not. But why bury the pregnant woman in the compost heap, holding an apple on high? Ah, I realized—to divert suspicion away from himself, of course, an ordinary man with good intentions, only so that I, the detective, would move on in the belief that the murderer was a person of weak mental disposition, an evil outsider, and who might that be? Not the girl in the green coat, never, because she stood out from the crowd in a positive way, didn't reek of the same inflamed stench as the other mannequins. We're keeping all possibilities open, I said out loud—perhaps we were dealing with a female murderer, who hated the victim for her looks, the way she flexed and enhanced her beauty rather than played it down, in fact looked down on anyone less beautiful, offered herself to Tom, Dick and—precisely. A dissolute life, as they say. Was the green one in danger? The next on the death list?

Dear God.

I pushed back my chair, pulled on some long johns, even though it was midsummer, thick socks, my waterproof trousers that were lying on the floor, a woollen sweater, a sweatshirt with a hood, a briefcase, then ran down the stairs, pulled the metal detector out from behind the coats and thrust my feet into Father's running shoes to make my feet look big. Wait, I turned in the doorway, put his wellies on instead, it was humid outside, the pressure was low, which affected all the insects, the midges seemed heavier, the bumblebees flew closer to the ground and buzzed all the more, and by the time I got to the scree, it was pouring with rain and thundering too. Damnation, I exclaimed when I discovered that the neighbourhood boys had occupied the best spot, because there's no end to what one can find, if one knows how to look, in peace, concentration, crouched down with tweezers, a flashlight around one's neck, a runny nose. I wiped the snot away on my sleeve, struggled to tighten my hold on the tweezers, to tease a shard of glass from the crack, or possibly a piece of porcelain, because didn't they find a broken porcelain vase at the bottom of the victim's laundry basket? The components of porcelain are kaolin clay, quartz, feldspar, was it moulded? What was the finish? Oh, it was such a nuisance trying to see in the rain, the water got in the way, the cold gusts. I put the flashlight in my mouth, held the piece up in front of me in the discoloured light—but that's questionable, I murmured, spat out the flashlight, it was questionable if the piece could be linked to the young girl's lodgings. No, it was impossible to write in the wet notebook. The pencil lead broke as soon as it touched the page, dissolved. You have to move, whatever the case, the boys shouted. After all, I was sitting in the middle of the pathway, did I want to be killed, or what? I most certainly do not! I replied, and with somewhat clumsy haste, I gathered up my things, tucked the metal detector under my arm, and used the briefcase as a shield when I bent down under the dripping branches. Should I perhaps bribe them with empty bottles? There were empty bottles in the shed with a total deposit return value of more than just a few coins. They could spend it on sweets, firecrackers, Lord knows what. No. Instead, having thrown together a mid-morning snack, I now returned empty-handed, with a hidden camera under the front of my jacket, a ball-point pen behind my ear, and renewed determination, you can be certain of that, I said, as there had been some sensational findings in the lab, considerable amounts of particulate matter in the victim's blood, grit in the stool samples—now how would you explain that? There was nothing for it, I jolly well had to turn the whole place upside down, their crowbars, the jack, and the pathway as such, I said. That's what you think, they said in their mocking manner. I wouldn't be able to do a search, not just like that, if that's what I thought. In fact, they demanded I fill out an application form first. An application form? You call that piece of paper there an application form? Well, then we'd better pretend that it is a form, hadn't we, I said, and squatted down to sign the scrap of paper, using my briefcase as a hard surface. Do you have a ballpoint pen? No? It turned out the one I had behind my ear had run out of ink. Or wait, hold on a tick, I had a reserve in my jacket pocket, borrowed without consent from my mother's pencil case. So, I said again, brushing some sand off the paper and putting the tip of my pen on the first question. That's a very odd use of a comma, I said, and excuse me, I said, but does that mean that I have to describe myself in just one word? That's right, they said. Well, let me see, I said, and considered kind and inquisitive, before choosing observant, yes, observant was what best described me, because, as Father has said, I have an exceptional, almost unique ability to observe. The boys scowled at me. What I see with my eyes, I explained, microscopic details that very few others notice, small pixels in the air. Yes, believe it or not, I said, with the aid of a magnifying glass or other magnifying instrument, I could separate pollen grains from the rest of this organic soup, which broadly speaking is composed of bark particles, prehistoric algae spores, I see meteorite remnants in the rain, nickel ore, isotopes with various amounts of neutrons and chemical characteristics. If you like, I could pick out a razor-thin insect leg from the muck on this sliver of glittering, metamorphic gneiss. When I did pick it up, I noted it was a moderately large two-winged fly. And as you know, I continued, the fact is that an object becomes grainy if you get too close. Why's that? was their surly response. Well, I said, and started to describe for them the anatomic structure of the eye, the sphincter, a part of the iris, which adjusts the size of the pupil in relation to the intensity of the surrounding light. You can test this at home with a hand mirror, look at yourself as you gradually move the mirror toward you. Or you can try here and now, by putting your face right up to this two-winged fly, right?

Because when it gets too close, you'll discover that only the tiniest amount of light can slip in from the sides. Your pupils expand so you can see the details better, the minuscule waves, the dry detritus and small red lice creeping around on the ragged wings. But as you see, most things just become grey and blurred when seen up close, even though the lens, an elastic circle that, together with the cornea, refracts the light onto the retina, and changes focus from distant to close, is no doubt working as it should. Thin threads connect the lens to the ciliary body, a kind of backup, one might say, which changes the shape of the lens by tightening the ciliary muscle, which reduces the pull in the threads so the lens curves. And this so-called accommodation, that's to say, the lens's ability to curve, diminishes with age, which means that the ciliary muscle is weakened as a result of increased stress, which means that you can't train your way to better eyesight, boys, you'll just have to accept that only particularly gifted people are able to see the microstructures, even though the ordinary retina that you have been given is composed of one hundred and thirty million sensory cells, better known as photoreceptors, which can in turn be divided into two main groups, in other words, light-sensitive rods and colour-receptive cones, both intended to send impulses via the blind spot, which has an optic nerve made up of a hundred thousand nerve fibres that go from the eye's posterior pole through the optic chiasma where it creates synapses with new nerve cells that are then sent on to the visual cortex in the occipital lobe where the received information is sorted, processed and interpreted. Another thing you should know is that the space between the lens and the retina is filled by vitreous humour, a kind of gel-like fluid mass mixed with fibres and immune cells. And if there's a degree of blurriness here, it's often due to age-related changes that cause lumpiness in the tissue and cast shadows on the retina that look like blobs, spots, spiderwebs, which often occur along with other age-related symptoms, such as, well, creaking joints, stiff muscles, nothing dangerous, like standing on an unstable stepladder looking up through the hatch to a dust-infested loft, according to one of my old relatives. Get a move on, the boys said. Was someone humming? Impossible to judge who it was, as they all had clenched lips. Well, apart from the one to the far right who took a piece of crispbread out from a clear plastic bag, crushed it in his hand and threw the crumbs into his mouth. But before I forget, I swiftly continued, I should mention the yellow spot, or macula, a concentrated cluster of photoreceptors, hence the terms sharp-sighted and central vision, as the yellow spot is meant to depict objects that one looks at directly, though for the normal population, *cough*, there are only colour-receptive cones in this area, that's to say, no light-sensitive rods, and close up, the colours in the squashed fly will be shadowed by the face, so you won't be able to perceive them as normal. What? Yes, yes, I'll get a move on, I said, and ran the pen down to the next question, which I felt compelled to query, because did I really have to answer who I was in love with? What-has-that-got-to-do-with-anything? Everything! the boys said firmly. And if I lied, they would be able to discern my trickery by measuring the temperature of my asshole. That's the most ridiculous thing I've heard, I said, but I would be honest, all the same. If they would only be kind enough to stop their humming. And why did they point toward the forest? Huh? Well, standing there in the dark was my grandfather with his stick, how opportune. He smiled at me, or that's to say, it's not always easy to know, as the corners of his mouth always point down, even when he smiles. In his right hand he held up something shiny, which, on closer inspection, proved to be a polished agate with bands of carnelian, beautifully coated with glossy varnish. Later, Grandpa! I shouted. So, back to the matter at hand, who-am-I-in-love-with? Let me see, I said, chewing the end of the pen, it has to be the girl in the green coat. Who is she? they asked. A peripheral friend, I replied.

The same afternoon, just after five o'clock, the brassy, burgundy broad came barging into the office with yet another of her witness statements. Her kisses were wet, pressing, she spread her legs on the desk, held me firmly by the ears. I can't, I finally managed to blurt out before I—argh, let me go. I shook her off, turned away. I stood with my back to her for several minutes, my hand against the wall.

No, I would not allow myself any further escapades, imagine, these girls didn't even have real breasts, just lots of toilet paper that they tore off in long, whirring reams. And the burgundy babe, she never gave up, became hysterical if I didn't let her roll her menthol tongue around in my mouth, might even threaten an overdose, empty a bottle of fluoride tablets, only so that I, God help me, would put my hands on her breastbone, do a hundred compressions a minute, and then pinch her nose, clear her airways of vomit and breathe, breathe, breathe into her mouth until her black lashes fluttered. The victim, she sobbed, the victim took me seriously without looking stupid, Karsten. She saw a pale oak in the mirror, she said. Who? The victim? In a drug-induced high she saw a copper beech, she said. Are you talking about the victim? Oh, Karsten, she pleaded, got down on her knees and opened the buckle on my belt with her mouth. Damn it, now my father's calling me for supper, dammit Janet, leftovers, pork chops. I'm coming, I shouted. And so as not to lose the lead I was following, I chose to do it all in character, stomped down the stairs, ate like a detective, weighed down by work, overwhelmed by case notes, pushy women. Are you acting? Mother asked, as I summarily cut and launched into my chop. Ha! As if it were simply theatre, as if I were merely rehearsing, immersing myself in sensations such as warm and cold. There have been a few performances like that over the years; my mother drags me along to the community centre to see the local theatre group walk around on the floor, wearing white gloves, in fluid lines that flow into each other, no interruptions, no angular shapes, they turn on a heel and come back. Each to their own, I said, and put three forkfuls in my mouth at once. It's important that you look at Irene when she talks to you, Mother said. Yes, yes, one should look at Irene when she babbles away, has porridge on her cheek, a bib over her dress, tears in her eyes, when she, aaaah, good gracious, struggles to say whatever it is she wants to say, look how adorable, has to put down her porridge spoon to say it, as though she knows that words become more sincere when you struggle to say them. Are you listening, Karsten? my father said. Hello? my mother said. Are you in there?

The victim, the victim, I thought, reaching for the jug of water, couldn't see the connection between the victim and the swirling dust, well, pass me the water jug then! I barked at my mother. We don't give orders, Father said. Or actually, I said, it doesn't matter, I said, because I didn't have time to drink, had to work out an action plan, a budget, so thanks for the food, I said, and grabbed a packet of waffle biscuits from the kitchen counter before I ran back upstairs, up to the room where she, damn it, was waiting for me on the edge of the bed with her white legs, toes and crossed knees sticking out from under the burgundy coat that had slipped off one of her shoulders. Blasted mannequin. No, I had not missed her, had to work, had to be clear, firm with her, frankly ignore the fact that she wiped her eyes, the black mascara running over her fingers. Saturday, I wrote, fourth of the month. Bad weather. False tears. Ten days since the body was found. The one friend more seductive than the other. The most shy plays on her shyness. The most brassy on her brassiness. The only trustworthy one is the cool girl in green. But they all, including the one in green, say nothing when questioned, just giggle with a hand in front of their mouth—yes—unless they're munching waffle biscuits and twisting on the chair, so the crumbs fall between us in peculiar patterns. How about turning the room into a young woman's bedsit? No. This was when I realized that if I really wanted to understand how women worked in their strictly private minds and hearts, I would have to take a closer look at my mother, perhaps even interview her. What makes you happy, Mother? Theatre? What makes you sad? What makes you hopping mad?

In order to create a more relaxed interview atmosphere, I dimmed the lights in the living room. In a calm voice, I asked my mother to lean back, find a comfortable position, preferably put Irene down on the floor, at least remove Irene's hands from her face, turn her around. Irene can play with the woolly sock for the moment, I said, and pulled off the second of the pair of socks over the wineglass that I held by the stem up to my mother's mouth like a microphone.
I should have been more thorough in my

preparations, I realized, as my mother was rigid in front of the camera, and she replied with all sorts of nonsense about the seasons and small joys. The summer, she said with a forced dreaminess, as I yawned and zoomed in on a pimple on her forehead. The summer? Yes, summer makes me happy, Karsten, as does spring, the buds that bloom, the autumn, the particles of decay in the air, in the leaves, in the compost; she sneezed, held a handkerchief to her nose, leaned forward and ah, ah, ah, sneezed into the microphone. What do you mean by small joys? I pushed, wanted her to be more concrete, go into more depth. But it didn't work, her answer was mundane, something boring about opening the mailbox, opening letters with a knitting needle, opening the middle page of the Saturday newspaper, opening things in general, a box, a wardrobe, running a hand over her sundresses, the fridge, drinking something sour, vinegar, lemons, and boldly confessing that she often took a forbidden sip straight from the carton of juice. Super sour, she said to Irene, and savoured the taste in her puckered mouth, with a wily smile. No such thing as boring, she said, as she went through the pile of bills, signed various contracts, message books, pressing the pen down firmly to begin with and then gradually l i f t i n g allowing her signature to disperse in three loose loops, like smoke. She chewed her underlip to show her concentration, assessed all the English tests equally, no preferential treatment, pressed the nib in and out of the ballpoint pen, wrote a six, a red scribble in the corner, five, four, exclamation mark, *wrong preposition* in brackets, something about a paragraph, check quote, plus, minus, plus—Karsten! she called, asked me to get the caramels from her bag out in the hall, the brown one, no, check the other bag then, the net bag to the right, yes, that one, yum, she said, and tore off the wrapper, felt a pain as she chewed, she groaned, the caramels tugged at her fillings, yes, a shudder in her lower jaw where she, due to brushing her teeth too hard, had damaged the enamel. I want to see. Irene too. Yes, then she folded down her lower lip, like a curtain, let me film the calcified plaque along the edge of the gum. Minerals attach themselves to the plaque and harden, I said. Did you know that the calcium and phosphates in our spit crystallize, Mother? Diamonds are overvalued, by the way, nothing more than carbon, burn like firewood at seven hundred degrees. No, she had never tried tobacco, with the exception of Oliver Twist once, she admitted, when I asked her for the third time. What about spirits? Had she ever tried to get drunk on spirits? No, you know what, she said, because she thought that was enough now, wanted to stop the interview. But what about music? Did she like rising or falling melodic curves best? Messiaen, perhaps? Overlapping violins? You know, *Quartet for the End of Time*? No, enough is enough, and anyway, she had to leave soon, was going to meet the girls in just under an hour. Are you going to a bar? All these questions, she said, and lifted Irene up and passed her to Father as he came out of the kitchen with soap bubbles on his upturned sleeves. It was his turn to put her to bed. He held Irene on his arm like a ventriloquist's puppet. And she sat there kicking with her arms and legs while Mother reeled off a list of lullabies he should sing. She mustn't suck her hand, Mother said firmly, and Irene immediately pulled her shiny, saliva-covered hand out of her mouth and entwined her sticky fingers in my father's beard. But the most revolting thing I filmed that evening was Mother parading around in nothing but her underwear, the scar at the base of her flat stomach, skid marks in her cotton panties, not to mention the protruding moles on her back that Father no doubt stroked when they—no, the thought brought me dangerously close to vomiting, I mustn't think. Just look into the viewfinder, don't think, I thought, as I snuck along behind Mother down the hall to the bathroom. Thrusting her chin out, she leaned in toward the bathroom mirror and used a pair of tweezers to tease out a, yuck, threadlike growth of, well, keratin, presumably, and tallow, small black grains. Blurgh, she said, dryly, if not to herself, then to Father in the shower, because, wouldn't you know, she noticed my eye in the crack in the door. Oh, she said, when she finally discovered, after the rest of us, what she had in the middle of her forehead. She rolled up onto her toes into the light to look properly at the round bump with a yellow head that she then, having assessed if it was mature, popped with a needle, and pressed out the turbid pus with the tips of her fingers. She groaned, rinsed the gunk off under the tap, shook the water from her hands. Then she doused the wound with alcohol, squeezed out a white grub of ointment from a tube, put it on the pimple and stuck on a small, round Band-Aid. What was that? I took half a step back and turned the angle rotator to capture a soggy pile of clothes in the corner, but was careful not to lose the shower cabinet in the blind spot. Condensation clouded the mirror when Father stepped out of the shower. Did he say something? I didn't catch it, something about Irene? Me? Whatever, his mumbling was drowned out by the rubbing sound created by Mother clearing the condensation with a hand towel in zigzag movements across the mirror. She stuck a cotton swab in her ear. With her head tilted, she carefully turned the cotton swab, looked briefly at the brown wax before using the other end to clean the other ear, and with a *swoosh*, she threw the cotton swab in the bin, the lid of which opened when Father pressed hard on the foot pedal. Oh no, heaven help me, now she was going to sit on the toilet, she undid her trousers, stood with her feet apart, pulled at the thread that was dangling down from, oh gross, her genitals, a triangle of wiry grey hair, and out came the most revolting thing I'd ever seen. What the hell was that? She dropped it into the toilet with a splash, wiped away the smear of blood from inside her thighs while I, goodness, wondered if Father took it so well because he was a doctor, he was whistling as though nothing had happened, took a pair of scissors out of the drawer and started to trim his moustache. Move over, she said, pushing him to the side with her elbow, because now she was going to file her nails. She slipped the file in under the sides and worked, as they say, toward the middle, nail by nail, scraped out any dirt with the tip, chose the delicate shiny nail varnish, though only after considering the matte peach-coloured one that was well-suited to summer, but not to sunburnt skin, I thought, as she applied the shiny nail varnish with light strokes, precision. Will you help me with my outfit? she asked with a smile—she had lipstick on her teeth. Was she talking to me? What? Yes, of course it was embarrassing to be caught red-handed, that I was standing there like a numbskull behind the camera and spying on her. Will you help me choose my outfit then? she asked again.

Since you're asking so nicely.

Mother is a normal woman, that's to say, the kind who likes to dress according to the occasion, appropriately, doesn't like to stick out, but doesn't want to look too boring, either. She had four outfits laid out on the bed. I said that this time we should dare to experiment, be a little crazy. How about braiding her hair? Yes, why not? Mother said. But do put away that camera now, Karsten, she said. Yes, yes. And when she put on a blouse and an attractive summer skirt, with an elasticated waist, I suggested that she could zhuzh it up a bit by wearing a pearl necklace. I also put in a good word for her silver earrings, got out the camel leather sandals from a box under the bed, and as I got her approval for several more accessories, she looked truly super. Or was she not convinced? She twisted and turned in front of the full-length mirror to see how she looked, both front and back. I think I might have chosen a different colour for my tights, she said with her index finger pensively against her chin. It might look better with dusk blue to pick up the pattern on the skirt, she said, but I strongly disagreed. No, I don't think so, I said, because I firmly believed that the pale nylon tights showed off her calves to their best advantage. And it's a contrasting colour, I said, if not exactly the rage right now, Mother, it's timeless, bold. I would rather see the clear blue hem of the skirt against the deathly pale tights, hard on hard, the shiny silk blouse contrasted with a rough, homemade orange cardigan, and she should absolutely not put her arms in the sleeves. Just let it drape over your shoulders, Mother, like a shawl, I said, and pulled out the bags from their shelf in the wardrobe, threw them onto the bed. The black clutch bag, I said. It's perfect, I would definitely have chosen the black clutch bag,

I said, if only it wasn't so small, there's barely enough room for a lipstick and car keys, you'd have to carry your wallet in your hand, Mother, and that's a bit risky given the many slippery-fingered pickpockets who tend to get in the way. Go for the beige leather bag, I said, because it's big enough and has a pocket with a zip on the inside. You certainly know your stuff, Mother said. You're a real pro, Karsten. No, I wouldn't claim to be a pro. I do have good taste, I said, a sense for what's elegant and what's not, but I don't want to waste all my time and energy on fashion, Mother, as I have other more pressing interests, among other things, detective work, a complex murder case. Oh, tell me more, Mother nagged. Well, I said, with some hesitation, and took more time than was needed to put all the bags back on the shelf in the wardrobe, one by one, the most expensive furthest to the right, kind of elevated by all the others. Or why is the most expensive always the most exalted, I thought, and changed them around so the cheapest appeared to be more exclusive than the rest. Hello? Mother said. Let's just say that I'm toying with the idea of studying law in the future, I said. Law, you say? In order to become a deputy judge, to be specific. But only after completing my compulsory education and then three more years of further education, something I must say I'm very much looking forward to starting, as, according to Father, I'm likely to end up in a class with at least one personality type that matches mine. She looked at me, as though she thought I was holding something back. It doesn't need to be a full match either, I said, I'd be happy as long as I don't end up in the same class as the boys from around here, as the last year has been unbearable, in fact I would go as far as to say that the only thing that has kept me going in any way is the thought that I will sentence them to prison as adults, whether it's for drunk driving or other worse crimes, like, well, violence or drugs on the open street, the latter being most likely. No, Mother, I think you've misunderstood, I said, they don't bother me, I lied, it's just the constant surveillance, their crude, social jargon, quick one-liners, shoving, raucous laughter, often centred around a punctured ball that's passed aimlessly between them. And, I said, drawing breath, as regards

the murder mystery I'm working on, that's preoccupying me at the moment, there's a victim, yes, she was found stark naked, in fact. Stark naked? Mother said. Ooft, I shouldn't have said anything, this feels ridiculous, her eyes were wide open, as though in shock.
I noticed now that her blouse was very tight around her wrists. And even worse, the skirt was see-through from behind. The seam of her underwear was visible from a good metre away, in fact, cross-stitch, flowery border, and excuse me, but I wasn't going to stop her going out and parading around unknowingly in front of people, feeling terribly chic. Promise to keep me updated, she said, cheerfully, before hurrying out to the ladies who were waiting in a taxi in the drive. Was there anything else? She got into the passenger seat, rolled down the window and called to me, as if the information she'd just been given was not confidential, that she was looking forward to hearing more about the body in the morning. So now she appeared to be curious about the case, new leads and developments. Over the next few days, she asked me, as often as the opportunity arose, if there were any updates, if I'd managed

to question all the exes, what they had to say for themselves, would I be finished before the garden party, by the way? How about showing my detective film to the neighbours? We could take out the screen your father uses for his slideshows in the basement, make a proper open-air cinema, sit on cushions on the grass, serve apple cake, wouldn't that be fun, eh, Karsten? Um, I don't know, not so sure, Mother. And then there was a day when she absolutely insisted on seeing what I was doing at my desk, wanted me to explain every single piece of evidence, no matter how small, dirt from the stool samples, the passport photograph, etc. What on earth does that piece of crispbread signify? she asked, and I apologize for saying it, but she was really starting to get on my nerves, the way she leapt up in anticipation, like a fool, every time I opened the door from my room. No, I was not allowed to lock the door from inside, in case of fire. If only she could knock on the door! Stop harping on about the damned garden party all the time! And then it happened, as I was filming a critical scene, she told me off in front of all the neighbours, young and old, for having laid Irene out naked on the compost heap with a bottle of beetroot juice.

She had gone a step too far.

For want of a key, I had to push the bed against the door, lift the chest of drawers onto the mattress, and turn the basin taps on full. But I do knock, Mother called from outside. No, you don't wait for permission, you knock then walk straight in! I shouted. And and and and I no longer want you to kiss me on the cheek in the morning, I get too much saliva on my cheek and sometimes your mouth brushes the corner of my mouth when you do it! But isn't that kind of nice? Mother said. No, it makes me feel sick! I shouted. And and and and I don't want to exchange pleasantries in the morning, either, or make my bed, say whether I've slept well or not, I just want to eat in peace at the end of the table, away from the rest of you, because you actually have to respect the fact that I don't want to talk before I've had something to eat, read the newspaper and drunk my coffee. So, you drink coffee now, do you?

my mother asked, as if that was something new. Oh, I groaned, banged my head against the wall. Stop it! Mother said. Do you know what? I said, I will hereafter be allowed to go to bed without saying, without having to say thanks for today and good night to you all. I will light the candles on the windowsill without having to ask for permission first. And and and and I will decide what time I go to bed myself, in fact I would like to have a contract, because now I want to come and go as I please, like an adult, it should be up to me, because because because I don't want to compromise myself any longer! Compromise yourself? Mother said. Yes! I shouted. We will meet for meals and go to bed at the usual time in the evening, Mother said. No! I shouted. But Karsten, we like being with you, you see, Mother said. We think it's fun to be with you. It's not mutual, I shouted, and now, well, I knew I might regret this, but unfortunately I didn't have time to regret it there and then, I could regret it later, because now the wind was howling outside, the branches were rapping on the windows, and if my reading of the cloud formations was correct, there would soon be a full-blown storm.

And it came as fast as forecast, a dark and sombre thunderstorm. The detective, whose office was at the centre of the storm, had just lit as many as one, two, three, four, five, six, seven, eight and twenty candles when a rude concerned party started to hammer on the door like a mad person. Who could it be? To his great disappointment, it was the audacious young woman, unmistakable in her burgundy clothes, agitated, with condensation on her sunglasses, wet hair, she pushed past without greeting him, and immediately threw herself down on the chaise longue, as though she expected him to drop anything he had in his hands and serve her, what, water?

Was she thirsty?

Mmm, she said and reached for the glass that he held out to her. Coat first, he said, and lifted the glass higher. His hips creaked slightly as he shifted his weight from one leg to the other. She lowered her sunglasses onto the tip of her nose, looked at him over the frames. Was she challenging him to a staring contest? Well, she lost the competition, but her stamina, puh, he wiped a few beads of sweat from his temples, because her stamina was impressive, he'd give her that, the girl had willpower, that was not the problem, there was still some defiance in her smile when she finally took off her coat, damp and bedraggled, she threw it at him so suddenly that he almost spilled the water on the carpet. Sorry, she said, as he shook some leaves from the coat lining, hung it on a hook by the door, adjusted the loop so the fabric hung in fine folds. Was that swearing he heard? When he turned around, she was lying on her side in the fetal position, chewing her fingertips. Tell me, he put a hand to his newly groomed moustache and coughed, you don't happen to be under the influence of anything? It was her eyes that prompted the question, the pull in her eyes, those big, brown prying eyes hidden in the shadow of her glasses. He leaned toward her with the water, tried to see if her pupils were affected by the flickering of the candle flames or not. But then, her fixed pupils might also be due to nervousness, tense nerves, perhaps she was on the verge of a nervous breakdown, he thought. Poor thing, she was trembling like an overwrought soul. What was that? What did she say? Do you play chess? she asked. Chess? That was unexpected, he thought and drank the water himself, the whole glass down in one, because it was unlike her, an indication of hypersensitivity, wide-open filters, within seconds she'd assessed any potential threat, gained an overview of the room, the vase, the sink, the dressing gown with the words *Question everything but this statement* written across the back, his slippers, sports club certificates tacked on the wall with rusty drawing pins, the equipment on the desk, the cleaning fluid, fat, brushes, hacksaw, polishing rags, and finally, the chessboard on the bedside table, where the pieces were standing: king against queen, knights muzzle to muzzle, the bishop's diagonal route to the last black rook. Breathe, he said, reminding her to breathe. She should lie with her feet elevated, there were cushions in the cupboard that he could stack up under her legs. No thank you, she said, unbuttoning the collar of her dress.

Is that a cold rash? he asked, and pointed at her flaming red chest. Mmm, she nodded, drowsily. Remember to breathe. He drew a circle in the air, to represent a clock, but also a square—no, she simply didn't understand. First breathe in, he explained, and swallowed a mouthful of air. Then you hold your breath, he gasped, and slowly exhaled. Wait a few seconds before once again breathing in, he said, filling his capacious lungs before *poof*, he managed to blow her fringe out to the sides. Forget it, she yawned. Was she wearing a wig? No, forget it. Forget it? What kind of talk is that? Gallbladder talk? Exactly, yes, bitterness and bile, that was how they communicated, they were both fluent in this dorm language. Well, he'd forgive her that last comment, she who had just rebelled against any friendship patterns, opted out, told them that religious convictions like that were not compatible with a hectic everyday life. The one in green had fully understood her. But the others, puh, she couldn't be bothered to talk about it. No, you have to tell me, he said. Stop nagging, she whined, and put her hands to her face to feel if she was in her face or her face was in her. No one is hollow, he said quickly. We're in that secret space, he said. Oh, she couldn't bear to hear the truth. Soon she'd pulled off her nylon stockings, knotted one around her throat, felt her skin start to prickle, her lips become numb. And as if that were not enough, she pulled a sawed-off shotgun out from her dress. Where had she got hold of that? She put the muzzle to her temple and with a sharp *click* her sunglasses leapt from her face. But no danger, the shotgun was empty of ammunition. You should know yourself through others, he said. No no no, she said, I want to know myself in others. Boldly said, he promptly replied. You're a strong young lady, talk about mental strength, you've hereby demonstrated that, but whining doesn't suit you, he said, brusquely. So, he said, let's get that mess off your face. Yes, her makeup was smeared all over her face and it would in fact have been wrong not to say anything, not so much as a murmur about how ridiculous her face looked. He turned on the tap, filled a bowl, and with the other hand grabbed the nearest pen to write down all thinkable hypotheses as to the cause of her behaviour. No, the harm done by such behaviour need not be immediate, but over time it could lead to somatic health issues and disabilities, he explained. You have two voices inside you, he said. The one that wants you to choose wrong all the time. The other right. To the one that makes you want to choose wrong, you should say: Get behind me, do not contaminate me with your insinuations, *whoosh*, away, three times. And to the one that makes you choose right, you say: Thank you for always being strict, but loving, that is how I recognize you, even when you are strict. It's all about will. Willpower is the emotion of command, he remembered reading somewhere. One always has willpower at one's disposition. One obeys the will's orders and takes action accordingly, unless one is not *compos mentis* in the moment of action because a desire for revenge, power over others or confirmation of one's own excellence has got the upper hand. Yes, and that's how simple it should be in a democratic society, where law and order should and must be built on theories that are understood without difficulty by the layman. But, good heavens, what was she doing now? Looking at her reflection in the washbowl? You should wash yourself! he said. And the murderer, had the murderer killed the victim as a result of willpower or desire? Who was to know. He considered the causal relationship between illness and the ability to assess. Of course, mental irregularities should be judged by a doctor, but surely only a systematic detective was qualified to establish a relatively correct answer as to what exactly those deviations were from? Following a thorough appraisal of ethics, assumptions and well-documented effects, he chose to ask about the wig again. Hmm, she said, dipping her pouting lip in the water. There are no mirrors in prison, he said. Only thick concrete and plastic cutlery. A horror and a warning, he continued, the purpose of punishment, an intentional and desired evil, is to cause the ignorant suffering, so by the end of her sentence she's learned her lesson. And at the same time, the aggrieved get their revenge without having to break the law themselves. So it's win-win. The more serious the crime, the worse the punishment. But, he said, if you confess immediately, we can try to negotiate a lesser punishment. Huh? she gasped, with a horrified expression on her face that said: What are you accusing me of in the first place? No, it wasn't the murder he had in mind. It was the coat hanging on the hook, it didn't belong to her, it wasn't her size.

Let's call her the Coat Thief, he noted.

Exactly.

And as the name suggests, she was the sort who wore stolen coats in order to sabotage, stir up intrigue, misunderstandings, make you question who was who—as if detective work weren't chaotic enough already. How is it possible? he groaned. If it had only been the one instance, but he had scores of reports about her in his files. So, he thought, it's not just her protecting herself from suspicion, the truth is that she had nothing to do with the victim in the first place, but chose to get involved for her own entertainment, out of pure, cynical boredom. And he didn't have time for that sort of nonsense. No, he slammed shut the filing cabinet drawer, because the worst of it wasn't the complication and confusion she had caused, but that she'd stolen the coats from friends who trusted her, poor girls, yes, girls of slender means, who were proud of their coats, the little they owned, who clung to their coats, it was enough to bring tears to your eyes, yes, because he'd become fond of them, she must understand, even her, he'd become fond of her too, it wasn't that he was any less fond of her than the others, he was kind-hearted enough for that, but, hold on to that thought—what? What did you say, Father? Pick what?

You mean we're going to live on foraging, or what?

Gooseberries, you say?

And now he's all secretive again, jogging up the hill as if there's somewhere we need to be on time. I'd initially decided not to ask if we were walking aimlessly, or if we were moving toward an intended destination, a thing, a place, but what? What exactly was I doing in the bushes there? Well, I just wanted to check something, Father. Check what? Found a coin in there, I say, and hurriedly put it in my pocket.

Nothing to keep, no. But I have to say, it would be good to sit down soon. I think I see a good resting spot up there in the clearing, a viewpoint, there's a small shelf on the slope where we can sit down on spruce branches and get that campfire feeling. This is quite a hill, by the way. No, I don't mean to complain, I'm just saying I'm working on an empty stomach, I mean, we didn't have breakfast, something Father has obviously forgotten, which is unlike him, he's the one who always says that I eat too little, plies me with three boiled eggs, grapefruit, cod liver oil, several glasses of milk and a slice of bread with cream cheese before I've even washed myself in the morning. In fact, when I think about it, I haven't been this ravenous since I fasted in the shed that time. A risky stunt, for which I was seriously chastised. Got a real telling-off from Father, a sermon where he, having broken in by unscrewing a wall, accused me of endangering my health and life. It's forty degrees in here, he said, and forced me to swim in the pond with my clothes on, pushed me out into the water. The fasting was actually part of the investigation, he should know. I wasn't doing it for fun. The idea was to understand the victim's desperation physically, with my own body, how she must have felt toward the end of her life crisis, when she was pregnant, with bulimic hunger pangs, and was forced to take modelling jobs to pay the rent, yes, quite simply to prostitute herself, Father!

It was the fourth of August. Misty. The clock had stopped on a sorry odd number, and the detective was showing obvious signs of stagnation. His breath smelled of acetone the last time he'd checked, his armpits of cortisol, and the ballpoint pen he normally took notes with so eagerly now felt heavy to hold. Should he ring the girl in green? To his great despair, he'd not heard from her for several days. And where was her telephone number? No, it was impossible to find it in all the mess on his desk, apple cores, test tubes, and what was that? A brochure about disorders of consciousness caused by self-inflicted intoxication? So, in the end, he spent the rest of the afternoon reading through old notes, paying particular attention to witness statements about house parties where the victim was constantly trying to be the centre of attention. Tiresome behaviour, according to the witnesses. She could hold forth about herself for hours, not letting others talk, jump from one thing to the next, almost without drawing breath between blows. And if people voiced their discontent, tears sprang to her eyes and she told them about all manner of offences that had caused her irreparable damage over the years, and so drew the attention back to herself again. She was a leap year baby, poor thing. Had only been celebrated every four years with miserable gifts from a missionary organization, wrapped-up rubbish, fake jewellery, good-luck trolls, a broken Mixmaster that gave her an electric shock as soon as she put the plug in the socket. The detective grunted, something wasn't right. Hang on a moment, perhaps it was the coat thief they were talking about here, he thought, and waded through the pile of patient records where the victim was described as being particularly introverted, closed, with clenched fists, hunched shoulders, the sort you had to draw and tease every word out of. Yes, it's true, she screamed at the psychiatrist once, that he mustn't leave her, but that was provoked by emotive slides of various stepfathers in singlets. So, the detective thought, the question is whether the real version is the timorous little sparrow who tried to protect herself from transparency in the therapy room, or if her true face was that seen at social gatherings when, with her girlish voice and wild arm movements, she drew on any appreciation and care there was to be had in the room. Who was who? He put a finger to his eye. He had recently noticed that people's faces as a rule comprise a dark side and a light side. That these sides enhance each other. If the right eye is big, the left eye seems to be disturbingly small. And all the expressions that appear to career across the entire surface in spasms, tics, trickery, seemingly complex but actually not, because they can only go up and down between the chin and hairline and in and out between the ears. He thought about expressions of joy, when the corners of the mouth lift the cheeks so the pressure at the corners of the eyes makes the skin wrinkle, which narrows the eyes, and so one raises one's eyebrows to open the field of vision from above. If, on the other hand, one is sad, or dejected or tired, the corners of the mouth pull down so the cheeks fall with gravity, as do the eyelids and skin on the forehead, without other muscles trying to prevent the field of vision from shrinking even further. And if the pressure in one's throat is painful enough, tears are squeezed out of the narrow, red-edged slits. Aggressive expressions were often rectangular, revealing the front teeth and gums. And then there were the more subtle emotions, such as envy, which tends to push the jaw forward ever so slightly. What about love? Well, attraction widens the eyes, the nostrils flare and the lips fill with blood, so the Cupid's bow stands out like a bridge. What was the Coat Thief's general state of mind? he wondered. Her face was expressionless, as a rule, almost impossible to tell what was going on inside. When she was in the room, when she was standing in front of him, staring at him, it was like being sucked into a black hole. When faced with something like that, it takes a lot to imagine what the person is thinking, based on what they're not expressing. The opposite is equally hard. In fact, it is enough to drive you mad. To-drive-you-mad. Strange, he thought, because the investigation, examinations of the crime scene, the conflicting witness statements, it was all starting to strike him as much more than a simple crime. Over the course of the day, he'd found himself thinking about the entirety of his life more than once, that the whole of him, the sum of who he was, if not more, had crumbled, no, not crumbled, had been consumed, precisely that, he'd been consumed by the Coat Thief, the victim, the green beauty, he had neglected his hobbies, friends, could no longer remember what those hobbies might be, or the names of his friends. Or, no, if he pulled himself together he could remember some escapade or other from the old days, a snifter that quickly became a couple of snifters too many, there was a group of them, an indefinite number of men who went out carousing together, played billiards, checked out the ladies, gave their backsides points out of ten, ended up in fights, dislocated jaws, he asked for more, asked to be punched, his friends held the ice packs on his shiners, sang forgotten broadside ballads, walked shoulder to shoulder, whistled at passersby, they were occasionally accused of incitement, but always defended each other, felt the brotherly love in those arms around their shoulders, stumbled over manhole covers, fell on one occasion, no, several occasions, yes, and the one pulled the others down as he fell, then it was on to the next bar where some braggart insisted on buying the whole world a drink, but who was that? Was he a friend worth keeping, perhaps? He couldn't remember. Who am I? he asked no one in particular and the answer was not forthcoming. That's the question, he sighed, and unfortunately had to acknowledge that, as of now, as impenetrable as this case was, he knew more about it than he did his own person. Ergo, he concluded that the imminent solving of the murder mystery would also provide the answer as to who he had now become. Exactly. Someone who couldn't let go, who was constantly entangled in new knots and charades in order to avoid the mystery ever being solved. He understood that now, and with that, his work took a desperate turn. It felt precarious. And his notes, idiotic, superfluous, the last two, in particular, that he'd spent disproportionate energy on reformulating:

The evening sun was, characteristically, low in the sky.

What is a house without a spire? A shack?

It was time to fast. I filled a large can with water, carried the can into the shed, and I locked myself in with a doubled-up chain and padlock. To block out any noise, that's to say, Mother fretting on the other side of the wall, I put on the noise-cancelling headphones that Father used when cutting the grass. Hell and damnation, my notebook was outside. Well, so be it, I had to prioritize now, trust that the notebook would be left to lie where it was, untouched, not to think about it anymore, just focus on what I'd begun, stay the course, get to the bottom of the victim's desires, dare to face her baseness, her animalistic instincts and vices that would become worse and worse as her hunger reached new heights. I dealt with the heat by imagining it was winter, ice cold, that I was sitting there with frosty breath and icicles coming out of my nose, great bouquets of them. When the nagging outside suddenly stopped, I pulled off the headphones and wrapped my t-shirt around my head like a turban. What was she doing? It sounded like she was dragging something heavy around and around over the gravel. Nope, now I couldn't hear anything. Hello? I put my ear to the door. Oh, God help me, it was here I recalled that I'd mentioned something about the neighbourhood boys harassing me on the last page of the notebook, that maybe Mother was reading it now. Oh, she mustn't read it, I hadn't left it there for her, if that's what she believed, no, the last thing I wanted was hysterical mothers getting involved in the mess. Don't read it! I shouted, but there was no response to be had. Perhaps she'd taken the book indoors? D-A-M-N-A-T-I-O-N. She would tell Father, close the door to the bedroom, talk in that hushed voice she used when she spoke common sense to him behind the wall, in their sweaty double bed. This calls for cunning, I imagined I heard them say. This calls for cunning, we must approach this nasty business with care, and ask Karsten about other things that apparently have nothing to do with what we really want to know, things that Karsten is enthusiastic about, things that make him so proud that he tries to hide the fact that he's proud, sucks in his cheeks, thinks that we can't see that he's proud, and you know how pride loosens his tongue, makes him chatter away about all that he's thinking, and we know how to pay attention to his chatter, we could, for example, start by asking what colour coat the victim liked to wear. Good question, I found myself thinking. Ach, I kicked a bucket. Why hadn't I thought of that before? Are we talking indigo? Almond-shaped, copper buttons? What was she wearing underneath? Only a veil? Was she a belly dancer? Where was the coat? Was she running naked through the forest? What was her running style? How big was her pregnant belly? Could it be that she swung her arms, perhaps hid behind a tree, waved her veil? What did it mean? Was she alluring? Huh? Bald? Was I seeing it from the murderer's perspective here? Was it his or her reflection? Was the murderer bald? What? Yes, speculation was important, building on one question after another, and to answer the last with the next, but not come to any conclusions, because I mustn't get bogged down by all the hitherto-ness, but rather open up the space, let the framework grow, yes, extend the radius in upward spirals, remember to keep the body in constant movement, threw myself against the walls, pulled out the lawn mower, picked off the coating on a knob for who knows what, stirred a rusty tin of paint with a stick, squashed a moth with a ski pole, scratched the ceiling, and I could probably have carried on like this for a few more hours, had one of those unexpected threats not been pushed through the crack under the door.

TO KASTEN. WE HAVE YOUR NOTES ABOUT VICKTIM. MEET? KIND REGAURDS THE ENMY.

So, the enemy had pipped Mother to the post. One less thing to worry about, at least, I thought, and ran a finger over the writing.

An apparently simple message, but reading between the lines I got the feeling there would be demands for a reward. And if I knew the boys right, a small symbolic sum would not be enough. No, they were greedy, I mumbled as my eyes wandered over to the empty deposit-return bottles that were piling up behind a thicket of fishing rods, life jackets, berry pickers, and yikes, they really did not wish me well, I knew it, wouldn't surprise me if it was the metal detector they were after, it was absolutely my most important identity marker. If they hadn't come up with something even more mean. In the worst-case scenario, Irene. Oh, what a dilemma, how hard could it be, the way I so recklessly downed the water from the can, spilled it on my clothes, and suddenly, oh buggeration, about halfway through the process, the whole point of fasting disappeared, yes, the original aim had been to better understand the victim. Instead I was becoming increasingly concerned about myself, at the cost of the victim, what's more, turning the whole venture into a kind of egotistical, psychological, spiritual experiment that involved recasting the ideal self as the actual self and thus making me into a sterling person, a tall guardian, the sort who never begs, who has no needs—was I seriously considering giving Irene away in exchange for a notebook, really? I had already proved myself capable of luring her onto the compost heap with an irresistible dew-blue celestine of strontium sulphate with rhombic symmetry, which she must in no way put in her mouth. I was a bad brother. Sanctimonious. Materialistic, not least. Was I creating a crime story to get rich, or otherwise? That Mercedes I wanted. All the time I'd spent looking for silver in the pile of scree, for bronze, for rust-red coins engraved with lilies, portraits of queens, screechingly shiny coins, while the boys killed animals at the edges of my vision, let the blood spurt everywhere, feathers and small bird squawks, why did I never say anything? Did I even have an opinion about such meaningless interference with nature? No, the only thing on my mind was the Mercedes, to save enough capital wealth in the form of precious stones bought and paid for by my grandfather's pitiful pension. Strangely, it felt nothing short of liberating to realize I was a useless boy. Because if that's the case, I thought, my dark side is of equal size. One might say that I confound the principle of contradiction by being one hundred per cent kind and one hundred per cent mean, I thought. The question is, which of the two reverse sides should one show to the outside world? The best, of course. But in order to be the best, the ideal has to be defined, calibrated, it has to be fine-tuned until there's barely anything left, and when the ideal is thin enough it should be given a final polish by means of a selection process where any unevenness is lost in favour of an ever-smoother whole. I actually wouldn't mind exuding something utterly undemanding, spartan, abstinent, aesthetical, no, I was not going to leave the shed until I had been transformed into an intentional person who could no longer be described as being controlled by the karmic wheel. And goodness me, the hunger was searing, the cold burning, and soon the jerry can of water would be empty too, I got the last drop of water in my eye when I held the can up with the spout to my face. Hunger heightens your senses, I told myself. Your tongue fills your entire mouth with metal. And your intestines tighten, forcing you to straighten your back, like a soldier.

Dehydration, on the other hand, makes you confused. For a moment there I slipped into a comatose state and drifted into a misty landscape, not too dissimilar to this. It could of course be that my memory is playing tricks on me, but yes, I do believe that I have been here before, in precisely this dead grass wasteland—or was it actually even grass this-this-this here?

Father?

Blimey, that's well, ow, that's well rooted when I pull at it, I tell you. No point in trying to pull it up. Wonder if it's sedimentary stone from the Cambro-Silurian period that's hiding just below the soil? A geologist once said that stone is chronology. And by that he meant that if the layers in a lithostratigraphic unit have lain undisturbed, one can assume that the earliest, oldest components are at the bottom, the next in the middle and the youngest, most recent, stacked on top of the mass of minerals, fossils and lime deposits. The chronological course of events must obviously have a starting point that is an objective, quantitative event, such as a volcanic eruption.

Another matter is that big, noisy events don't necessarily have more impact than things that happen quietly and go unnoticed, something I o f c o u r s e took into consideration when struggling with the dramaturgical headache involved in cross-cutting the crime material. The murder was the catalyst, yes, that's where the timeline started in this case. The course of events should follow straight as a piece of string, no, in loops, a noose, like a bow, a rope tied in a bow that somehow caught all the small details that had mounted up before the death. And these events, botheration, were numbered by date in the notebook that was still in the enemy's possession. I opened the bedroom window, called to Father. You'll have to wait, Father said, as he was repairing the wall of the shed, stood there hitting the corrugated iron with a sledgehammer. Regardless of my protests, he had chosen to remove the cordons from the crime scene. Can't look like that when we're expecting guests, he said, and wanted me to rinse the beetroot juice out of the grass. With the pressure hose, or not? I asked, from the window. No, he said, there was an age limit, as the pressure was so high that if the spray were to hit someone on the head or in the stomach region it could be dangerous, there was a risk that vital organs could be damaged. Really? I said. Forget it, he said. You can pull up the nettles by the pond instead, he said. But remember to use gloves, Karsten. I had to do it properly, he said, all the way to the edge, so it was safe for the children to sit on the edge with their toes in the water. And watch out for adders down there, he said when I eventually got myself together and went outside. I had never seen any snakes there, only a slow worm and that was ages ago, and now, blow me down, I found a dead magpie. Goodness, I said, and held it up for Father to see. Please put on your gloves, he said, without even looking at the magpie. Something long and revolting was hanging from its beak and it almost brushed my cheek as I balanced on the uneven and unstable slabs on the way to the compost heap. No, throw it in the bin, Father shouted, which I did, I threw the magpie in the bin with the rest of the rubbish, and when I turned on the hose to rinse the feathers and slime from my hands, I noticed something alarming lying on the gravel. Another envelope?

YOU LOOKING FOR WORD TO THE PARTY? YOULL GET BACK YOUR BOOK THEN. BUT ONLY IF GIVE US EXSACTLY WHAT WE WANT!!!

The detector. Yep. Of course. Unless they meant my stone collection? Irene was not an option. The period of fasting had in fact knocked a little sense into my head. I was, for example, more patient, didn't even get annoyed when she played the grand piano, dribbling, when she hit the keys with her sticky hands. I even let her play with the evidence whenever she was dumped in my room because Mother had to go to the toilet or had an important phone call to make, or the like. But please don't touch the stones, I said and quickly explained that it was in fact quite difficult to get rid of fingerprints. She could look, but not touch; there was a perfect cube of silver that she'd fallen in love with, reached up to the edge of the desk. No, don't touch the washbowl! But she drank the soapy water from her hand as though it were a stream. On another occasion, she put my long johns on her head, and bent over, as if she had legs at either end, imagined she could walk on her head, waddled off with her diaper-clad bottom up in the air. I'm sorry, I don't have time for this, I was in the middle of cross-cutting, I really didn't have time, I shouted to Mother, I shouted,

MOOOOtHER!

Hold on a moment more, my mother answered from the bathroom. And when she finally, after a good half-hour, lifted her babe up from the floor, she didn't say thank you, but rather that I had to contribute to family life as well. What do you mean? I collect the mail every day, take out the rubbish, do the weeding whenever anyone asks. And who was it who volunteered to fillet the fish on Tuesdays? I asked. Because, you see, it was me, and she knew that only too well—that it's Karsten who fillets the fish every Tuesday, opens the newspaper carefully in order not to tear it, holds the fish by its belly, makes a cut behind the gills, throws away the head, puts the tip of the knife in the anal opening, draws the knife along the backbone, puts his hand into the opening, gets hold of the innards, twists until they snap, pulls out the entrails, scrapes away any blood from the cut, removes the skin, holds the tail, lays the blade of the knife flat and draws it forward until the skin loosens, food for the seagulls, they're tapping at the window, the skin billows if I talk with my mouth close to it, but this is where Father takes over, because he is apparently the only one who can divide it into fair shares—what? No, I can't dissect the entrails, it would make too much mess, stains on the newly polished wooden countertop that can't be scrubbed off, he says. And when I ask what that white stuff is that's seeping out of the liver, he replies that some things can simply be left to the imagination, Karsten. Grandpa found an engagement ring in the stomach. Puh, is my father's response, and he turns on the tap, holds my fingers in a hard, cold stream of water as he rubs them with dish soap, picks the bits of shell out from under my nails, says that I have to shake off the water, that it's not always necessary to dry your hands on the towel. He turns on the gas cooker, lights one of the burners with a Zippo lighter, drops a lump of butter into the pan, tells me I can put the fish fillets in the frying pan when the butter is bubbling. One at a time. Yes, one at a time. One lump of butter for every fillet. They should be fried until they start to curl and go brown around the edges. He throws in some salt, grates lemon zest over them. It needs something green, I often think. It's somehow a bit flat with just potatoes. Well, out you go and get some parsley from the garden then, Father says. Parsley, is that all? Once I'm out there I seldom pick only parsley, I take in some lovage as well, stalk full of leaves and shoots that we only use a fraction of in any one go. There's no need to overdo it, Father says, he so easily tires of the taste. No, I can only use the tiniest amount and that's more than enough, so my next job is to put the rest of the stalk in the tallest vase I can find in the cupboard. What have you got in your hand? he asks and chuckles every time. You're a one, Karsten, he says when he discovers it's a fish eye that I'm squeezing in my hand. Did you pick that out of the rubbish? Yes, haha, I'm a one, Father. Then I have to wash my fingers again. But there's no need to be too meticulous about it, Father, is there? I say. No, he replies and puts a whole pile of plates in my hands. Whoa, I say, collapsing under the weight, and shuffle hunched over into the dining room, put the pile down on the table with a thud, and, ow, notice the red marks on my hands, that my fingertips are yellow, numb, have no feeling, and now I can't remember on which side the forks should be laid, if it's left or right, I should remember, Father has told me so many times, that the fork goes on the left, the knife on the right with the blade facing the plate, and the dessert spoon along the top with the handle facing, um, left or right? Right! Father calls through. And then there's the napkins, which I make into swans, even though Father shouts that triangles are good enough for a Tuesday. Well, he can think what he likes, I think, and follow the step-by-step instructions: First fold the corners into the diagonal middle line, then turn the napkin around and over, so the middle line is vertical. I then fold the two long sides in to the centre so the diagonals lie at right angles to each other, before smoothing out the wrinkles, and in that way create a perfect diamond with two longer and two shorter sides. No, the rest of the process can't be explained, I say when Mother comes in and shows an interest, has no doubt been standing behind me for a while, that's how devious she is, wondering how I do it, apparently impressed by my art, but sorry, it can't be explained, it's just in my fingers, it's automatic, when I pull the end, roll the neck, form the beak from the tip, lift two loose thirds to make the wings, tear the corners to make a fringe and, ugh, never happy with it, have to start again, again, crumple the napkins up, it can take forever, it doesn't matter that the food's getting cold, have to get the balancing effect right, that the swans are balancing on one foot, making the fringes quiver, seemingly delicate, and yet robust when subjected to pressure, damp, awkward fumbling, because then they should grow in your hand, swell like sponges when you drip water on them. How beautiful, Mother says, but takes away the five-armed candelabra that I actually need to see what I'm doing. Don't take it, I say. Well, she's afraid it might start a fire, even though I've promised not to set fire to the swans again, we both remember what happened last time, that it ended with a hole in the tablecloth and a whole lot of drama, mainly because I ran away, fled, but not too far, no, I sought asylum around the corner with Grandpa, who was having an afternoon nap and was so grumpy to be woken that he demanded I return to whence I'd come immediately, take responsibility for what I'd done, apologize to Mother, which proved to be unnecessary, because before I'd managed to say anything, Mother said that she was sure I hadn't meant any harm, even though it was stupid, it wasn't bad, and there was a world of difference, Father said, whereupon

Mother listed all the stupid things she'd done in her life, that she'd skipped school, tried cigarettes—oh, really? What kind of cigarettes? I asked, but Mother had barely voiced the first letter of the brand name before Grandpa rapped his stick on the kitchen window, shouted that he was sorry, that he had been too hard on me, he said, and wanted to give me a semi-precious stone to help heal the wound, an agate dyed with chromic acid, as if I was fragile and needed a Band-Aid, as if I couldn't cope with a telling-off, have you seen all my sports club certificates? Oh yes, we have, they all said at once. Well, I don't believe you, I said, and got them all to come up to my room with me, where they, instead of reading what had been said about my achievements, stood and stared at the small cotton wool balls on my desk. What on earth . . . said Mother. Well, then I had to tell her the final details of the case, and resolve the many misunderstandings that arose whenever Father, an expert know-it-all, said anything about the victim's diet. For example, he thought it was very troubling that the victim was in the habit of sucking cotton wool balls dipped in—what kind of concentrate? Broth?

Exactly.

Balls of cotton wool soaked in broth.

If one were to believe her medical record, she stored the cotton wool balls in her cheeks or under her upper lip, like a tobacco pouch. When she pursed her lips, the cotton wool fibres were pressed together and the salty fluid was squeezed out and spread over her furrowed tongue which she then moved, flipped and twisted, so the taste sloshed up to the hard and soft palate, the nasopharynx and the epiglottis, which vibrated when she gurgled. All the sucking and slurping made her diction unclear, hence the spittoon mug. During their therapy sessions, the psychiatrist held the mug under her chin. Perhaps you should give your mouth a bit of a rest, he tried to persuade her. But that was out of the question. She always had to have something there. Always? Yes, otherwise she dropped out. Of her mouth? Exactly. And then there was all the water she drank, which the psychiatrist believed was in some way ritualistic. She had a self-inflicted saline imbalance as a result. Well, on the positive side, this imbalance made her more receptive to hypnotherapy. He put on Messiaen, but first pressed the on-button on the amplifier that should ideally be left to warm up for five minutes, but, well, never mind, he carefully put his hand into the record cover with the back to the paper. By cupping his hand, he created enough space to reach his index finger to the hole in the centre. Where was it? He searched in the dark until his fingertip finally found it, and gently eased the record out. Puh, he said, blowing the dust off the underside of the record, put it down on the turntable, lifted the pickup arm, moved the needle to the right track, no, not the sixth movement's unison dance of rage for piano and cello where time goes backward like a demon at top speed, no, not the unbearable sadness of the fifth which at its peak pierces the heart like a baby's cry, but the slow eighth movement for rest, reconciliation, fundamental misgivings. He fished a ticking pocket watch out of his breast pocket and held the chain with two fingers. Follow the movement, he said, adapting the swing to her pulse rate, which beat slower and slower as she slipped deeper and deeper into a blissfully relaxed state of peace and calm. Now the images could come, the confidences, her innermost, strictly secret young-girl dreams. Tell me, he said. Wait, she murmured. Can you hear the hum? she asked and waited a while before whispering that the hum came from the crowd. She was one of many people inside many, many people. And how does that feel? he asked, moving closer on his chair. Hmm?

Did you say something, Father?

You're a bit of a whimsical prima donna, aren't you? No, I'm not slacking on purpose, got blisters, that's why I'm so far behind. No, no point in looking at my heel, it's the collar of my jacket that's rubbing, I say. Look, the zip rubs against my philtrum when I talk. Wait. Hold that thought, Father. Please don't distract me now. I'm sorting and tidying up my thoughts. Give me a couple of minutes, just going to hunker down here for a moment, try to get the threat letters in the right order. You're asking how many? Hmm, there's been quite a few now, one two three, no, I would hazard a guess that the total number to date is somewhere in the region of seventy-seven, in fact. Where do I keep them? Not in my room, no. If you really must know, I folded them into swans, put gravel in their wings, which made them sink to the bottom of the pond. But I remember them off by heart, Father. Yes, no problem, as they're so short, easy to remember, especially the one that was put into my back pocket when I was using the metal detector to look for an earring that Mother had unfortunately lost in the scree.

TIK TOK TIK TOK. THE CLOK IS TIKING. FROM THE ENMY

The evening sun was hanging low in the sky, as evening suns are wont to do. Mother had put out cushions on the grass, lit the lanterns in the trees, and the freshly baked apple cake was on a red, checked tablecloth, in front of the maid, who was wearing an apron and head scarf for the occasion. What fun, Mother said, as the maid was supposed to look like she was serving behind the counter in a cake shop.

No comment, I said. Now, remember to greet everyone properly, Father called from the kitchen window. Shake them by the hand and say welcome, he shouted. Yes, yes, I said. And as expected, that's to say, a whole three-quarters of an hour later than stipulated on the invitation, the guests tumbled in through the gate in a flock. Welcome, welcome, I said. Diction, Father coughed, and nudged me hard in the ribs. Yes, yes. W-E-L-C-O-M-E, I said, and shook everyone by the hand. Complimented the ladies on their dresses. Showed the men the way to the bar behind the shed. Yes, because there was alcohol for the adults, soft drinks for those underage, but at some point in the evening, the person keeping an eye on the beverages was not attentive enough, and the neighbourhood boys managed to sneak some bottles of alcohol, beer, which they poured into their glasses, and spirits as well, certainly from what I could see.

Is that Kalinka you're drinking?

Yes, I have to confess that I had a taste, as I've never claimed to be innocent, but it was only the tiniest amount, barely a sip and *cough*, aye-yai-yai, *splutter*, huh, that sip was enough to put the fear of God in me, I spat it out and retched, and could not understand how the neighbourhood boys happily managed to pour the amount they did down their throats. How can you bear to, I said. The responsible thing to do would have been to tell Mother what was going on, and I did consider it, but having weighed up the pros and cons of snitching on them, I concluded that I shouldn't disturb Mother who was laughing and having a good time with the other women over in the corner of the garden. No, not Father either, as he was inside changing Irene's diaper, or the snotty one as I called her in front of the neighbourhood boys. Go on, take a sip, they nagged. It gets better, promise. Thank you, but no, I said, because of my migraines. What are migraines? they asked. An intense, booming headache, I said, but Father says I'll grow out of them. Everything's spinning, one of them said. You don't give up, do you? I said. C'mon, Karsten. You'll get your notebook back if you down it in one. No, this is starting to feel like peer pressure, I said, and I felt it, goodness me, the pressure was such that I nearly gave in. But then Father came out through the veranda door with a bundle of cables, thank goodness, he shouted to me that it was time to start, we could set up the screen and get ready to watch the film. The boys retreated as he approached. Soon they were standing over by the edge of the forest, hiding the bottles behind their legs. This is sporting of you, Karsten, Father said, clearly nervous on my behalf. But if there was anyone who was sporting here, it was Mother, I thought, I'd give her that, as she'd agreed to lie on the compost heap in a bikini, and more, earlier in the day. Without her, the crime project wouldn't be complete; there were still some flaws, true enough, but I thought they were just charming. If I had to point a finger at anything, it would have been the scene where the victim scrambles over the scree, crying. Yes, because Mother overacted here, I thought. Another weakness was that she was supposed to be a young girl, so her grey hair didn't fit. But no, I didn't have the heart to say that, as she had given it her all. She really went for it. The way she crawled over the scree as I threw water over her, buckets of water, she stretched her hand out toward a protruding rock, something to hold on to, an edge, but everything was slippery, she scratched herself badly, reached for the Gravenstein apple, couldn't get hold of it, as the water and mud were pouring down over her, and goodness, how she cried. Oh, how she cried. She cried and she cried. Her grey hair hung down in wet straggles over her face. She cried a beardful.

Cut! I screamed.

Puh, she said, blowing the dirt out of the corner of her mouth. Not sure that I can face any more takes now, Karsten.

One final take from the opposite angle?

I think it's good enough now, Karsten.

Yes, so we wandered home again, me behind with the camera on my left shoulder and all the buckets on my right arm, Mother sauntering in front with a pair of laddered tights in her left hand. When she got into the bath and leaned back, the water turned brown. But Mother, I said, pulling back the shower curtain, we're not finished yet, I said, because she had promised to play the body on the compost heap. You're right, she sighed and hauled herself up from the water, limped over the floor tiles and sneezed as she snatched up the carefully selected bikini that I threw to her. Bless you, I said. You're not allowed to go through my drawers, you know, she said, and tousled my hair. Less of the pouting, Mother! Sorry, she said. This time it would be a good take, no matter what, yes, just as anticipated, with grainy shots of two worms intertwined in a knot along the bikini line. Cuts and grazes on her knees. An ant in the corner of her eye. It was powerful stuff. Unfortunately, we never got as far as the decidedly most powerful scene, and that was entirely the fault of the neighbourhood boys. And let me tell you, I wasn't the only one who reacted to their jeers during my introductory speech, but they didn't seem to care that people were shushing them. At one point, they made so much noise it was as if they were having their own party within the party, a completely separate party where anything was allowed, be that burping, cackling, cutting one's mouth with a cake fork, climbing the tree, roaring with laughter, pushing and shoving and chatting and drinking themselves into new states of consciousness, that's to say, jumping over at least five stages until boom, they found themselves in a new state of consciousness, swaying in timeless forms. And this, this without having to do the crazy amount of work that in reality is needed to rise up the ladder.

YES, it's called laziness, it's called weakness, palatable drinks that run out again as white piss. I should have filmed them, made sure to document them throwing up in the flower pots. And poor Mother, who, tired and bent over, had to pick glass up from the grass. And by the way, it has become a recurring discussion between Mother and me, as to whether it was she or I who first suggested the outdoor screening. That it was me? Mother firmly believes that it was me, that I orchestrated the event, how the apple cake would be served, etc. Whereas I, for my part, seem to remember that it was she who came up with the idea, she who persuaded me, who used the expression

“oUtdoOR ciNemA.”

Honestly, and it's the God's honest truth, I was not at all interested in showing my work in progress. I wanted to make the crime film for my own use. Really. The idea was to watch it in secret, show it to my closest family, if necessary. Surely, they knew me well enough by now? Karsten? I have never been someone who begs for fuss and attention. No, I'm more the sort who keeps themselves to themselves, intensely present with my metal detector in my own mysterious thoughts. And the introductory talk, well, surely she didn't believe I enjoyed it when, on her explicit instruction, I simplified the more difficult things, given that there were children in the audience. Explain cross-cutting to a child. Make it engaging, use silly voices, sign language, move your hands like scissors, not even an idiot would enjoy doing that. Well, let me tell you, I said, and with that I moved on to a topic designed to impress the older audience, the ones who knew how to appreciate depth, weight, in other words, what best describes geo (earth) and logy (knowledge), because they should be aware that in the magnetic field between total confusion and a fully resolved murder mystery, I had snuck in a couple of interesting facts about the origins of the earth, how various materials raced in circuits around the sun before clumping together into defined orbs, planets, moons. If they were interested, I could give a brief explanation of the entire process? Mother shook her head, whispered something to Father, but the other adults nodded enthusiastically, responded with a resounding yes when I asked if I should go through the process step by step, the whole of evolution, from that big explosion in space to the point where raptors wriggled out of the dark, salty sea. Yes! But before life began, the world was desolate, I said, barren, I said, bare rock, high pressure, soaring temperatures, shaded streaks of brown, scarlet-red sunsets, corrosive acidity levels made the water uninhabitable, flames erupted whenever the magma rose up from the dark depths and forced its way into the sedimentary deposits of shale and granular sandstone, which in turn were covered by layer upon layer of shiny, black lava, like a glaze. The ground shook, if not as a result of a meteorite shower then as a result of tectonic plates colliding and folding in the ocean currents, as mountain ranges were pressed up from the creaking substratum. We're talking massive mountain structures, crevices that branched out into fractal networks, thousand-metre-high blocks that rose up sideways in forests of cones, pipes, pyramids, pots of boiling gas, sparkling streams. The first micro-organisms gave the pools a greenish tint, stones rolled and rumbled in the depths as sulphuric winds blew over the water. Oh, this is all wrong, I thought, as I could hear how much information was being left out when I went at this pace, I had to slow down if I was going to illustrate slow time, the slow drift of the continents, the heavy, basaltic composition of the ocean floor, how the environment became favourable only then to be wiped out, complex ecosystems that dried up, froze to ice, burned up or melted, before plants and animals were reborn in more or less sustainable variants. Grandpa should have been here by now. I lifted my arm, looked at my watch. Mother appeared to be losing patience. What did Father think? Should I show the numbered samples? Take out the suitcase and let those who wanted to feel the feldspar powder that had been found in the bite mark on the apple? Now, who was that humming? Shhh, I said to the neighbourhood boys. Shhh! The most important thing, I said in a voice loud enough to arc over their noise, the most important thing is to view the stones in the context of the crime scene. Feel free to smell them, taste them, run the tip of your tongue over the grooves, please chew the magma flakes, feel the crisp biscuit consistency between your teeth. Now, this is a curiosity, a jasper stone from abroad. In the far box you'll find hexagonals, tetragonals, along with an illustration that explains the crystallization process. And this grey stone here is a typical representative of the stones found in the scree. The relative age can be calculated based on the general rule that the lowest layers are oldest. And with that in mind, I continued, the change in colour from grey to red is a characteristic of the transition from Permian to Triassic. Permian is grey, Triassic is red. The red colour is due to rust formation in the topsoil. But, I said, nothing is guaranteed until the elements have been studied under a microscope. The samples are either pulverized or sawed into slices called thin sections. No, lab work is not for everyone, one has to be pedantic by nature, enjoy chatting about isotopes, measuring half-lives, cleaning off grimy contamination with cotton swabs, fatty remains, water molecules, have the patience to trace the lead content in a piece of hair, for example. And speaking of lead, mass spectrometry is used in the lab to measure differences in the masses of various elements. The mutual quantity ratios reveal the age of the mineral grains. The younger the minerals, the more lead there is. However, the method doesn't function so well with minerals that have a high uranium content, as the radiation extracts the most important elements needed for dating. The potassium-argon method can also be used, or the rubidium-strontium method, or carbon-14 dating, just to be clear. Psst, Mother said. She used her hand to cover one side of her mouth as she whispered that we needed to start the film soon. Well, I said, I hope you'll all have an interesting experience, but I must warn you that it may seem like the detective forgets to solve the murder mystery toward the end. This is because he chooses to invest what capacity he has left into other things altogether, such as fusing his scientific obsession with geology with a more romantic philosophical twist, which, on a mental level, ends with him being thrown out into the atmosphere, which allows him a full overview, and almost by chance he understands what killed the victim, that's to say, what tightened the hands around her throat, which she-devil squeezed the living daylights out of her and did not let go until the colour of her bald head changed from beige to purple. There was a raw edge in the air. And the she-devil, a hawk of a figure, balanced on her creaking stiletto heels across the night grass, before disappearing into the forest after casting a yellow eye back over her shoulder. The footprints smelled of piss. Clouds of particulate matter spilled out of her black coat pockets. She was the storm itself, a nightmare to work with. She sometimes pretended to be someone else, wore a wig. But she wasn't alone in this, as dressing up as someone else was something everyone did. Because the point of the film, I said, is that everything that appears in the world is an expression of the same being. When the psychiatrist removes a fleck of ketchup from his doctor's coat, when the detective uses tweezers to pick clues out from the synovial membrane, when the mannequins hold a memorial service at the scene of the crime, they pout their lips and accuse each other of being fake, but it's always oneself one struggles with most. It all boils down to the same being. The hints have been there, an avalanche of fluoride tablets. One can visualize a compost heap crawling with larvae and flies which each see the compost heap from their own unique perspective. When the victim clambers up the steep slope, it's actually the burial mound that mounts her, and to the sound of a grand piano in the distance: a cross-eyed little girl who presses down atonal minor chords with her sticky palms. The little one's eyes roll around in their sockets. There is sea and sky. She loves her fingerprints, dribbles on the piano keys as she sings coded messages to the particularly observant harlot. Yes, the harlot. A portrait of a moon-pale queen in a gold frame. And one might well ask what on earth does the apple signify in all of this? Well, I would encourage you all to draw a cross on top of a heart on top of an anchor and see what it becomes. You will find pens and paper under your cushions. And now, all there is left to say is: Start the film!

It was night and it was dark, and the moon was full when the detective rolled in from the right in a shell-grey Mercedes with moonshine on the hood. She didn't notice him at first. She stood lost in thought on a street corner, veiled in blue cigarette smoke. He rolled down the window, asked for her telephone number. The tip of the cigarette crackled as she inhaled. He coughed, with his hand to his mouth. I've managed to lose your telephone number in all of this, he said. Tell me, what's your number? he asked once again.

One, she replied, with some hesitation.

Nine, she said, with a tentative smile.

Six, she said, and bit her lower lip, provocatively.

Three, she said, and flicked her hair over to the other side.

Two, she sighed, putting a finger pensively to her brow.

Or actually, she giggled, I really meant two, three, nine, nine.

Speak soon, he said and sped off. But then looked back. Because he couldn't just drive away from her, not now that he'd found her. He slipped into reverse, turned the wheel and sped back, slammed on the brakes at the corner and hello, hi, he said, drumming his fingers on the handbrake, he wanted to take her with him now, right away, because I've made up my mind, he said, he had to have her, I have to have you, do you understand? She seemed doubtful to begin with, or perhaps she was just playing hard to get, delaying, but then finally—after much umming and ahhing, back and forth—she got into the back seat, like in a taxi. Where are we going? she asked. Well, he said, lacing his arm around the headrest on the back of the passenger seat, putting all his weight on his right buttock as he reversed east, then suddenly changed gear and headed west, away from town, out toward the sea, a long and winding road, a deserted bend that led into another bend and on into another, and another, bend after bend, the bends were the winding road with high seas to the left of the car. Can you help me, she said, unable to find the buckle for the seat belt. Good heavens, does that really matter? Feel the freedom, he said, and she heeded the young man's advice, got up from the back seat, opened the roof, poked her hands and head out, stretched her arms up into the air, let her coat sleeves flutter, so free, like flying, she shrieked on the bends, got salty spray in her eyes, the tears streamed, the tears streamed down her cheeks and ran out to the sides and then together again on the tip of her chin like a heart, his tears too, his tears streamed like a heart out over the steering wheel and the Mercedes veered from side to side because he only had one hand on the wheel, and with the other reached back in an attempt to support her so she wouldn't fall over on the sharp bends, he reached back further and further and further, without taking his eyes from the road, felt her skin was as soft as silk, that her thighs vibrated whenever there was gravel under the tires, oh, oh, she said when his hand slipped up under the fabric of her coat, he swung into a bumpy side road, parked by a tree she thought she'd seen before, perhaps in a dream, a tree with roots at both ends, she said, synchronizing with his thoughts. We think the same, he said and deactivated the safety lock, whereupon she jumped out of the back seat, took off her coat (she was wearing a slip underneath), took off one shoe, then the other, she ran backward out onto the sand, her shoes in her hands, one shoe in each hand, waving her shoes, she staggered out into a wave that crashed over another wave, then she fell into the water, the sand disappeared from under her feet, sucked the shoes out of her hands, they disappeared into the undercurrents, oh, oh, oh, she let herself be swept along, dove down for her shoes, grabbed her shoes, poured water out of her shoes, stood up in her see-through slip, her breasts were pert, her nipples blue, her hair flowing, an extension of the waves, a hand of waves, black below, moonlight above, she tossed her head, tossed her heavy black hair up toward the moon, like pillars, high, ah! he gasped, could barely breathe, she took his breath away as she spread herself out, yes, in such a way that only she was prominent, and a singular sound rang out like a random perception process. It was sorcery, he thought, if not divine, virginal, because she had communicated directly with his subliminal perception, made the material insignificant, the car invisible, where was the car? Have I driven an invisible car?! And now he could no longer see her either, a passing system of water and lips, couldn't see anything properly, had the sun in his eyes, no, the moon, to be painfully precise, was he being forced to reassess his perspective, or what? Perhaps not to take it for granted that the self was the perspective? Oh, what does it matter, what does it matter, now he just wanted to swear on all fours that she was the right one, the only one, the last one, even though it could never be a mutual obsession, no, she was the law, he was nature, he had no choice, like the bearded one on the cross, a premise that time and again nails the human son to the structure. Oh, dear God, now she ran her fingers down her belly, slowly took off her lacy underwear and he swore on the rose, the sea's inside-out fruit, which according to an underestimated magpie is kind enough to lend its rosy hue, he swore on the sea air, a scrolling text of snail shells up the dunes, he would live in this ecstasy, breathe her in with all that that entailed of musk and rouge powder and that's enough of the humming now, I shouted, paused the film, damn and blast, the neighbourhood boys tore a page out of my notebook. Hey, hey, hey, where were they off to? I couldn't see which direction they ran in, because Mother was standing in the way, nagging at me to start the film again.

Move, I said.

And yes, of course, it was foolish, downright obscene of me, I must have been out of my mind at the time I committed the act, but there, at the far edge of the garden by the pond, I squatted down behind a bush, pulled down my trousers and shat into an envelope. On the outside I wrote: a thousand gorgeous rock crystals. The most important thing now was to get the notebook over to my side of the hedge before the neighbourhood boys discovered what was in the envelope. Yes, I had to think fast, play on the slim chance that drunken idiots were easy to fool. Listen here, I said, we can discuss the detector, if you just wait to open the envelope I've given you until you've thrown over my notebook.

What do you say?

Look, there comes my book, sailing over the hedge, leather covers flapping and page upon page of blotted pen ink. Right, I said, you're going to leave me in peace for the rest of the evening now. Oh jeez, I heard them say. Jesus, Karsten. And immediately regretted my actions, got the feeling things would get nasty now. Oh, Jesus Christ, this means war, Karsten, they said and came after me with their crowbars, hacked their way through the hedge flowers, so now all I could do was run, I ran for my life, out of the garden, into the forest, back and forth between the paths while I frantically looked through the pages of my notebook, running, licked my thumb every fourth sheet, couldn't find the last page, tripped on my damned shoelaces, got earth in my mouth, felt something pointed against my spleen and woe is me, I thought, because as soon as I touched my spleen I suddenly understood what the mannequins meant when they talked about holding back the pain, having to swallow it, what it means to hold back the pain when your daily life consists of withdrawal symptoms, miscarriages, I grabbed some spruce branches to hide behind, but botheration, I couldn't break the branches from the tree, and now the boys had seen me, they accelerated, thundered down the path like a herd of buffalo. We can see you, they shouted, I was besieged, finally, I might as well surrender now, they shouted as I folded myself up like an intestine on the ground, soon they were prodding me with their crowbars, wanting me to smell the contents of the envelope, and of course it revolted me, but what was I to do? What would the mannequins have done? They would have played dead. So, well, I did the same, I played dead and was surprisingly convincing, relaxed my muscles entirely, stared up into thin air, lay perfectly still, my tongue lolling out of my mouth like a dog, and there I lay, shallow-breathing through my nose. And the strange thing was, incredibly strange in fact, that I realized I was comfortable playing dead, unusually relaxed, I almost enjoyed it, listening to the fear, their desperate voices, all shouting at the same time, they didn't know what to do with the body, if they should wrap me in cling film, tarpaulin, roll me off the scree, perhaps? No, the loudest of them thought it would be best to scarper, some fifty per cent of the gang thought it was a bad idea, so it's a tie, someone said, but when they put up their hands to vote on the matter, it became clear that seven couldn't be divided by two, unless one counted half votes, or you could measure the arm lengths, the shortest to the longest, but then you'd also have to take into account the uneven ground, which was compounded in some places, and the fact that some of them were standing at the top of the slope, that the two shortest had cheated by building up their shoes with pine needles. Well, the slope was really too gentle to be called a slope, the loudest one said on behalf of the majority, a clear majority, he said over-confidently, he had no doubt, even though one couldn't be sure of anything here, because some of them reacted to the fact that two of the seven had crossed the line and votes weren't valid beyond the line, but what line? the majority asked, because according to them, that's to say, those who had just insisted on the line, the line could suddenly be said to be anywhere, in fact, it was irrelevant, they said, had never been important, because what had to be decided first was what was beyond and what was inside, and how could that be done without a line? What about a show of hands then? Shall we measure arms? From shoulder to fingertips, including nails? Who's got the longest nails? No, now all the votes on either side of the line were invalid, so the only solution was to draw straws, said the one who had been the first to criticize the line and thus influenced the rest of them, so they also felt a healthy scepticism each time the line was mentioned, but the

line

doesn't

exist! one of them screamed, and there I was, if not on the verge, then very, very tempted to make my own smart contribution to the debate. Yep, I almost suggested that even though the line didn't exist, one could still accept the line as an expedient means, that's to say choose to *b*

e

l

i

e

v

e in the line, that's to say, something to base the rules on, and when all's said and done, it doesn't really matter if SOMETHING SOMETHING SOMETHING

SOMETHING

SOMETHING

SOMETHING SOMETHING

SOMETHING

SOMETHING SOMETHING SOMETHING EXISTS EXISTS

EXISTS EXISTS EXISTS EXISTS

EXISTS EXISTS

EXISTS or not, it's only the rules that matter, in fact, we have to remember that game rules build on themselves to create structures here in the world. What's more, I thought, you can easily refuse to play by the rules, but a rule is a rule, and they can't simply be removed, because rules apply as soon as they're articulated, then they can't be ignored, denial only makes you sick, it's as good as poison, as rules are wont to become tyrannical, when they're left to grow in the subconscious without opposition, there's a risk that the dark side becomes stronger than the enlightened side, in which case the imbalance might eventually be dangerous, no, it doesn't help to change the name of the rule and believe that in doing so you can avoid the whole issue, one should deal with rules as consciously as possible, just that, no matter what your opinion of the rules is, on one side of the line or the other, I thought, and was about to elaborate on this theory when someone said that I was the line. Yes, Karsten is the line! In an instant, they were absolutely euphoric, jumped around in delight that they'd found a solution that satisfied all exalted parties. Well, what can I say? I would describe it as fairly momentous, for me too. Thank you so much, my heroes, I said, as I too was emboldened by all the endorphins and stood up, which I clearly shouldn't have done. Were we not standing in the same field of unity? No, the faces that stared back at me all wore an unequivocal expression of zero tolerance. Evil eyebrows. Several of them demonstratively held their noses. The one to the far right used his crowbar to scratch his chin. And someone even yawned, as though the situation was endlessly tedious, which was hardly the case, as a lot was at stake here, they all knew that, certainly for me. You can have the metal detector, I said, I'll be that generous. But it wasn't the detector they wanted. What is it you want of me then? The rat, they said. They wanted the rat behind lock and key. And the rat was obviously me, because it was me they pointed to when they chanted rat, rat, rat, even though I'd never told on them, had perhaps thought about it once or twice, but had never followed through and actually told on them. Explain this message to your mother, said the loud one, and pulled a sheet of paper from his trouser pocket. Well, I said, it wasn't really serious, just something I wrote in a moment of confusion while I was fasting in the shed. Rubbish, they said. No, listen, I acted on impulse, I said quickly, my heart hammers just as hard when I do something nice as when I do something stupid. But Karsten, your heart doesn't hammer very hard when you're unconscious, someone said quietly. The loud boy waved the piece of paper. You've written to your mum that the enemy is going to kill you, Karsten. Well, I can only apologize, I said, I'm sorry, sorry, there was no other way out than to beg for their forgiveness, though it didn't help, they had decided, they were going to put me in prison, but what about my rights? I had the right to a fair trial, the normal procedure where three professional judges decide on a sentence based on the verdict of a jury who are instructed at the outset to allow any doubt to fall in favour of the accused. But the jury thing has stopped, the loud one said, the sentence is now decided by two professional and five lay judges. I did a head count, and the number was good and true. I was in deep now. We all agree that you should be sentenced to life, Karsten, they said in one voice. Remember that remorse should outweigh the many mistakes we make, I swiftly reminded them, we mustn't be ruthless here, I said, and added that, despite being the one who had to atone this time, I wholeheartedly believed that society was safer thanks to our modern authorities choosing to invest considerable resources in fining and prosecuting the mad folk amongst us. Yes? Yes, I actually quite like the archetypal prison cell, a real human trap with bars, and undernourished prisoners who have to beg the guards for supper, only to have some thin soup and a piece of hard bread pushed through the bars. Because we need extremes, I said. Yes, these polar extremes should basically be as defined as possible, otherwise it's too easy to make allowances and cause confusion. But, I said, what I do find problematic is when the sentence is packaged as care, as if smiling guards make a prison sentence less daunting, when they ask, yuck, kindly if the prisoners want to play Ludo, for example, that's just nonsense, synthetic, lies, when evil is done in the name of good, I said, thinking I was being clever. They sniggered at me. We don't play ludo. You can't trick us into playing ludo with you, Karsten. Why were they whispering? Were they playing telephone? Huh? Well, whisper away then, I said, I'm just happy as long as you're not humming! I shouted, and made a sudden U-turn, yes, fled like a genius, one hand on my spleen, the other in the air, my notebook in the third, my knees were high, as high as my eyebrows, it's all about turning, twisting and turning so your coattails flap, first to distract, coax, manipulate, then *whoosh*, one runs like the wind, away from the rabble, the ground carries you upright, it's about trust, nothing but trust, mastering one's points of gravity, get them to fight for you, not against you, but swing your arms, pull up into your upper stomach, when the path loops just blink quickly to create a black-and-white effect, it's about trust, now, hang on a minute, the only thing I dare trust is what I can reasonably assume, I understood that, and what I can reasonably assume is, as a rule, based on banal trivia, I realized, and thought about everything from my shoe size to, well, let me see, which brands matter when I go to the shop for Mother and need to find the fabric softener with the fewest allergenic ingredients. My feet are growing uncontrollably. That's for sure, I thought. Thirty-seven is far too small. And the cleaning agent bottles that Mother swears by, the only thing one could say for certain about them is that neither the list of contents nor the apparently detailed product description tells the truth, certainly not the whole truth, I asserted, and what on earth is he doing here, eh? That was timely,

I must say, because there in the middle of the misty forest stood Grandpa swinging his stick. Had he been following me, or what? Was it possible? I mean, no one likes to be followed, he should know that. NO, I don't want any more of those stones of yours, I said, and repeated it several times, that I didn't want any more of his stones, because he's deaf, he doesn't hear what I say, that I don't want any more stones, no, not the precious ones either, Father. I mean it. I'm done with such childishness—what?

Are we going over the fence?

But how?

Run and jump?

Which opening?

Yes, yes, Father, I'm coming, just need to adjust my sock first. No, I'm not dawdling on purpose, I've told you. No, take that hand away, I'm standing steady here, see, stable on the steel wire, have tracks on the soles of my shoes that are made for steel-wire balancing. Stop fussing. Will just draw my stomach in with an inhale, hold it in, so as to pull the wave up from my knees, up through my thighs and hips, through my belly, chest, throat, face, then find a point to focus on, something fixed, unmoving, the tallest rush in that cluster over there. No, wait a moment, the rush is swaying, the oarlock in the rushes, keep a steady eye on that shiny point on the oarlock as I give it my all and swing my leg over the fence post, ow, don't worry, I'm in full control, Father, if you could just loosen my jacket from the spikes, stop, it's thorns, it's tearing, I'm stuck, you're pulling too hard, take your hand away, I say—how do you mean? No, give that branch, there, stop, I'll get a hole in the back of my trousers, no, let me do it myself, stop fussing, I'm waiting for the right angle, let the sun decide, twist with the axis of the sun, the reflection on the water, the flashing in the reeds, careful, hold the branch at an angle, no, don't take a picture, hold the branch at an angle like a slide that swings up at the end, hold on, because now I'm going to sit down on the post, ease the edge of the post into the coccyx groove until it says *click* and ta-da! slide down the branch, feet out, oh, oh, oh, *thud*, there, yes, that wasn't too bad, Father. Did it hurt? No, I wonder if I might have put my back out just a little. Nothing serious. Just an old neck injury from doing front flips at my sports clubs. Can flip until I'm sick. No, relax, I can sort it by shaking, like this, hands up high, must remember the ankles as well, shake it out. Stretching is important. The coach says I'm good at the step classes, by the way. You know, the aerobic dance thing with weights. Apparently, there's many an appreciative glance from the ladies' changing rooms. But like a true climber, I think I'm happiest hanging by myself on the wall bars. If the light's not too bright, that is. Can always ask the coach to dim the lights though. Would prefer it to be completely dark, yes. Hanging in the dark. Are you joking? We're going out in the rowboat? Why can't we take the path around? No, I refuse to wade out, I'm wearing my new denims, remember? Yes, yes, I could always take them off, but don't want to risk being seen in only my underwear by any passersby, surely you can understand that? Okay, fine, you keep watch then. Yes, shout if you see anyone. There, stand there, no, wait, I say, just some material that's got stuck in the zipper, have to tease it out without ripping it, wish I had a pair of tweezers so I could twist it, wait, that's it, clear, wasn't so hard after all, here are my shoes, socks, please put my trousers in a watertight bag before you put them in the top pocket. Whoa, whoa, whoa, don't shake them, I've got things in the pockets, just stuff I've picked up from the ground, yes, I know that, but I'm excited to see what I've got when we get home from our round trip. Huh? We're never going back? What about school? Ow, no, I didn't step on anything, I was just reacting to the water temperature, quite a shock, but now I've got used to it, find it almost comfortable, would guess it's around fifteen to seventeen degrees, oops, touched something sharp there, wonder if there's a scratch, no, it's fine, ow, *splash*, damn, *plop*, I slipped, I, Father, I'm soaking wet, so I hope you've got a change of clothes with you, because I'm freezing, see, my teeth are chattering, can you hear my teeth, *clack, clack, clack*, can you hear them? What? How did you get in, by the way? Father! No, I'm not shouting, Father, I'm just saying that I can't get hold of the edge, look, my hands just slide off, maybe you could pull me up with the oar? If I hold on tight to the oar blade and you pull me up over the edge? Yes, ready, I say, ready, steady, go, I'm ready now, have my legs crossed, hope that no one will see my wet-underwear behind, because they're see-through from miles away, well, come on then, I'm ready as an egg, all you need to do is pull and haul, no, the other way, I'll get splinters, spin me around, swing me to the right, there, yes, *ahem*, excuse me, but does this boat have a leak? The bottom smells of hydrocarbons. Fuel, that is. Isn't it called the sole? Oh, I see, it's the drips from the oars, right, typical me, make a mountain out of a molehill. You want me to sit down there at the front? But it's wet there. Can I sit on the bag? What? Is the outboard motor working? Have you pulled out the choke? Remember to open the valve on the petrol tank! No, I'm not shouting, I'm just asking you to wait until I've put on a good, warm sweater before you start the engine, just a tick, two seconds more, there: Now you can pull the cord, let's go, faster, faster, I'm no chicken, no, to the contrary, I want speed, excitement, give it all you've got, give me full gas, faster, faster, ah, the spray, talk about speed, I'm waving through the spray, you heard me right, because now we're heading out onto the water, the clear, open water, heave ho, the mighty waves, why am I waving? Well, what I'm trying to make a point of here is that we're moving away from the mainland, away from everything that's solid, I'm saying farewell to it all, farewell to the plains, to the hills in the distance, the bays, the cliffs, the corn-yellow fields, the poppies that line the country roads, horses and carts, an overturned tractor, two drunks in a bus shelter, they're waving, I wave back, high above the horizon, something black in the clouds, an ambulance helicopter that spins up from the urban exhaust and out toward the forests in the foreground, the paths, the lakes, over the two of us in the boat, an older gentleman and his waving boy, look, I'm waving through the spray, get a wave back from the pilot when he leans toward the east and swings his machine back toward the bustle of the city, the high-voltage masts, shopping centres, student accommodation, the main entrance to the university building that conveniently faces the better side of town, the reeds are whistling, the birds are singing, *tweet tweet tweet*, car horns honking on the highway, there are wheel loaders, cars, cyclists bumping over pedestrians crossing under bridges and into tunnels where the emergency exits lead into bushes with arrows to a shack with a payphone connected to a tangle of wires that twist up poles along the street between the houses, fences, dog-barking and, oh, poor Mother in there, behind the gate in the house in the misty conservatory, grey as a ghost behind the window, she blows through her lips, condensation on the glass, rubs away greasy marks with a worn rag, rubs and blows, but it doesn't help, there are just more and more marks, because I throw her a kiss with both hands, farewell, I say, and make the rose bushes lose their petals, the rain starts to fall, open mouth foaming, I don't know that I can bind the word to everything here in this world, no, I'm not shouting, I'm just pointing out that the concept is captivating, the table ensnaring, the fact that there's nothing that can't be left behind, could even leave the farewell if I absolutely had to, and I'm certainly not stingy, I spin it around me like a lasso, that's to say, a piece of rope with a noose, no, heavier, more like a slag-coated chain, rattling, listen, I let out the rustling cord, the end of which is a cross with a spear on its point that can cut through both this and that, coils around my inside and outside, my most important foundations, and oh, oh, oh, hangs me upside down by the feet, diggidy dang, I'm flying, I'm flying, I'm flying in upward spirals, rising melodies, see tree crowns shrink into tiny shoots, oh, but look, there's that volcano province I've always dreamed of exploring with a pickaxe, an enormous eye, oh, I can zoom in on the Areopagus, a woman who's standing on the protruding rock baring her breasts, I pick up some marble at the same time, put my hands into a cyclopean wall that blocks any view from outside, but not from above, I see it all, through the umbrellas, even into people's bathrooms, the expressions on the faces of those sitting on the toilet, that they, haha, out of pure curiosity look down at the lumps before they, ach, sigh, throw the paper they've wiped themselves with into the

toilet and pull the flush so the clumps spin
around in chlorine and swooshing sounds are
pulled down with hell-like suction into the
depths of the sewers where the rats dart under
and over and in and out of the corrosion-
resistant steel pipes, I see it, there's always
a chink, a hole in the ground, down into the
pipes, up into skirts, but now I want to
concentrate on the old woman who's getting
herself ready for bed, look at that, she puts
a towel to dry over the edge of the bath,
scratches her acne scars, picks a crumb out
of the toothbrush bristles, a bobble off her
nightdress fabric, a small golden drop into the
toilet bowl, frets that maybe the stain can't be
removed, can't be bothered to scrub anymore,
turns off the light, pads toward the bedroom,
her hair dragging behind her, long as a cape,
heavy as a trailer, she complains about her
sciatica, seems suitably sad that the day is
done, that she'll never experience that day
again, perhaps just as well, she yawns, topples
down onto the edge of the bed, pulls a hairnet
over her hair, pushes in the odd tuft, lays her
head down on the feather pillow, draws the
duvet dusty with mites and skin particles up

over her old, feeble, shrunken body. Then she folds her hands in prayer for peace. Our Father, who art in heaven. Forgive us our trespasses as we forgive them who trespass against us. And just listen to her snores, mouth open like a young boy. I wave from the mud. Look at me, Mother. It's Karsten. I'm completely self-sufficient. Yes, look at me now, I say, and flick a wood louse from my earlobe before I say my thanks and farewell, stroke myself on the cheek.

About the Author

Ingvild Schade received rave reviews for her debut novel *Drammen Book of Records* (2014). Schade has attended the Hordaland Art Academy of Creative Writing and writes both novels and plays. In 2020, she received the Bjørnson Grant, awarded to "an author for whom there is reason to have significant expectations."

PHOTO CREDIT: Håkon Borg

About the Translator

Kari Dickson is an award-winning translator who specializes in Norwegian literature. Her work includes crime fiction, literary fiction, children's books, theatre and non-fiction. She is also an occasional tutor in Norwegian language, literature and translation at the University of Edinburgh, and has worked with the British Centre for Literary Translation, the National Centre for Writing and the Translators' Association.

PHOTO CREDIT: Kate Griffin